A. MADHAVAN was born in 1934 in Trivandrum (Thiruvananthapuram), Kerala, to Chellammal and Avudainayagam, who belonged to Kanyakumari district. His schooling in the Malayalam medium gave him an opportunity to taste Malayalam literature. His literary interest widened with the Tamil works of stalwarts such as Pudhumaipithan, Ka.Naa.Su., La.Sa.Raa., T. Janakiraman, Na. Pichamurthy, Ki. Rajanarayanan and Sundara Ramasamy. Over a period of about sixty years, he has created a large body of literary work: three novels *Punalum Manalum* (On a River's Bank), *Krishna Parunthu* (Brahmini Kite), *Thoovaanam* (Drizzle); three important translations from Malayalam: Malayatoor Ramakrishnan's *Yakshi* (A Mythical Being), P.K. Balakrishnan's *Ini Gnan Urangatte* (And Now, Let Me sleep) and Karoor Nilakantapillai's *Sammaanam* (Reward); two novellas *Kaalai* (Bull), *Ettavathu Naal* (Eighth Day); some literary essays and more than sixty stories. Madhavan won the Sahitya Akademi award in 2015 for *Ilakkiyach Chuvadugal* (Traces of Literature).

M. VIJAYALAKSHMI has translated Thoppil's *Oru Kadalora Kiramathin Kathai* (The Story of a Seaside Village). She was the librarian of the Sahitya Akademi Library for many years.

On a River's Bank is a story of ordinary people through an extraordinary narrative. Angusami, Panki and Damodaran have very different needs and yearnings. Panki, Angusami's stepdaughter, is ill treated by him because of her deformed appearance. She holds this sulking father in high esteem while she dreams of a saviour. Her dream approaches reality when a young Damodaran joins Angusami in his work of dredging and selling sand, and acts as a bridge between daughter and father.

The riverfront pulsates with chaotic energy with the blessings of Madan Tampuran, the god on the banks. Prolonged sand-dredging causes wounds in the river, forming deep pits in its bed, resulting in torrential flows during the rains. The business becomes increasingly hazardous, making Angusami believe that it is all due to the ill luck brought by the deformed Panki. During a day of heavy downpour, a boat capsizes mid-river and passengers are drowned. Panki is among them. Will she survive?

In what must be a rare and sensitive portrayal of an ugly female character, the author underlines that violation of the river leaves it ugly and invites retribution despite worship.

Published originally in 1974 in Tamil, *Punalum Manalum* is a path-breaking novel raising the issue of environmental degradation through overexploitation, long before this became a topic of discussion in India. An early example of what is now known as 'ecofiction'.

RATNA TRANSLATION SERIES

ON A RIVER'S BANK

A NOVEL

A. MADHAVAN

TRANSLATED FROM TAMIL BY

M. VIJAYALAKSHMI

RATNA BOOKS

First published in English translation 2018
(by arrangement with Kalachuvadu Publications)

ISBN 978-93-5290-752-6 (POD)

Published by RATNA BOOKS
An imprint of Ratna Sagar P. Ltd.
Virat Bhavan, Mukherjee Nagar Commercial Complex
Delhi 110009, India
www.ratnabooks.in

One

It was the latter half of the rainy season. The rains poured down the slopes of the eastern mountain chain, without pause. The clouds gathered into huge dark shapes that rose above the peaks within moments and pummelled the earth as rain.

The Kottaiyaru river foamed and swelled from an invisible cranny in the Mukkunni slope. Yet a stream, it tumbled down and rushed towards the plain. The waters frothed and sped through the bamboo forests and grass, and enriched the earth around the small villages. The stream became a river, like a maiden come of age, by the time it appeared at Kundan Paalam, situated amidst a forest of majestic trees.

There were no paddy fields in Kundan Paalam, surrounded as it was by tapioca fields, green forests and hillocks of red earth. The trees had been nurtured well by the river. The jackfruit grew lush and heavy, bowing down almost to the roots of the trees. Mangoes hung from the branches in generous bunches. There were countless Kamugu trees. The virgin river that ran red with the earth which it had collected earlier was a tamed flow by the time it reached the pier at Kundan Paalam. Kulsekaram, Konni and other towns were in dire need of the river's slush and water. So the lively river was halted at the Marudan Kuzhi dam. It let out its energy by pouring its overflowing waters into the gorge down over the sluice gates that resembled giant teeth. It sprinted forward again, dashing and frothing against boulders of elephantine proportions. After flowing steadily up to Jagati, it swerved around Paraichirai and flowed towards Nettur.

In its long course, the river earned more fame at the Paraichirai curve than the Marudan Kuzhi dam. It looked enchanting at Paraichirai – a calm and shallow sea. Here, the washermen worked in the areas demarcated for them in the ghat. Not far from the bank were lush groves of trees – varieties of jackfruit, mimosa and thetti flower bushes, with thick red inflorescences. The washermen's dwellings lay in the east as those of the tillers. The row of thatched huts stopped at the Mudippurai Devi temple. On either side of the temple were sugarcane and sweet potato crops. The Paraichirai bank of the river was a picture of perfect beauty.

When the river was not swirling with the muddy rains of the monsoon, the washermen's ghat pulsated with activity. The washed clothes were wrung and squeezed, then aimed so that they would land on a clean white cloth spread on a dry area on the bank. Boys who amused themselves in the river were often tempted to take a peek at this revelry in the air. 'Go away, you little lords! Take your dip when we drink our gruel... We have more work to do...' an elderly woman would shoo them off, her heavy pambadams shaking in her stretched earlobes. The donkeys made a cacophony of their own. In the bathing ghat, the boys would make boats out of the sheaths of plantain trees and send them afloat. They would somersault into the river from the rocks and swim boisterously, challenging one another. The washermen would throw choice expletives at them for muddying the water and ruining their work. After a sedate run of two miles, following the tumult at Paraichirai, the river reached Periyasalai.

The Periyasalai ghat was a spot of considerable interest. Along the mud track above the ghat, at Chinnavur towards the south, lay the cremation ground. This was a 'hinterland' of four to five square miles around the town of Periyasalai. The river flooded the Periyasalai ghat to enable the performance of death rituals. The bathing area for the cleansing dips was long and spacious. The river was a boon for the Brahmins of the Periyasalai agraharam. The ghat would become crowded very early in the morning. The Siva temple on the hillock was a witness to the nature of men's piety. Devotees would arrive there at the crack of dawn to take a peek at the women's quarters in the ghat. In this ghat, few observed any differences by way of caste and the river allowed no distinctions either.

The river moved out of Periyasalai with a reluctant farewell. As it reached Vallamedu, crossing Killipaalam and Buddhankottai and passing over bleached rocks, it was joined by a companion from the west, the Perumanaiyaru. Vallamedu is where the river earns its historical perspective.

Two

The Vallamedu riverfront looked on to an immense expanse of water, stretching ahead to as far as the eyes could see. A host of boats bobbed up and down on the huge undulating surface – boats with woven roofs or plain ones, boats stacked neatly with coconuts, like rows of grain in a corn cob, and boats laden with balls of coconut fibre. Most numerous were the sand boats that hunted for more and more sand from the depths.

Like a marketplace, the river was crowded. Trucks halted on one side of the iron bridge, with its black pillars. This was where the road curved. The trucks were joined by pushcarts and ox-carts. The adjacent woods had plenty of manjanatti trees, thick with leaves that were given to the cattle to chew on. A leaf-thatched shed had been erected on the edge of the river, beneath the cement planks of the bridge. Sand harvesting, the most important commercial activity of the inhabitants of the Vallamedu riverfront, was conducted from this thatch, in wholesale and retail. There were no books to record the transactions made here. The contractor's representative sat on a stool. One end of his veshti, the waist cloth that covered his torso and legs, was used as a cash pouch that stayed close to his body. 'A cartload will be about ten basketfuls of sand. That will cost eight rupees. You can get sand that is drained of water and is reasonably dry,' he would declare. 'I cannot offer a better price.'

'In Kollangodu, a cartload is twelve basketfuls,' someone would retort, on occasion.

'In Kollangodu? Well, you can run along with your cart a good six miles and buy there, not here. This is no Kollangodu sand. This is Vallamedu sand... Better than grains of paddy...' he would counter. 'You there, you, the short man there! Dump the sand near the jackfruit tree. Let the water drain off the two boatloads. Don't you see that it is sunny there? Countless times I have told you men not to dump the sand so close to the bank. A single shower will push it back into the river. And that will seal my fate.

'Here you can get sand, no bricks. You can stop the vehicle here and walk across the field. There... where you can see the kiln.'

A small distance away from the shed, the site of daily commotion, stood a tall Pala tree, as large and impressive as a banyan tree. A cement platform had been built around its sturdy trunk and an idol of the village deity, Madan Sami, had been installed on it. A stone lamp, black with oil, stood in front of the god. The figure of a snake god stood close to the lamp. Nearby stood a brass pot for the collection of coins, which were offered mainly by the sand buyers, sand diggers and load carriers. The riverfront deity, Madan, was known to be a god with a good income. But more popular than the pecuniary aspect was the belief that Madan was a god who never failed men in distress. The god received lavish celebratory sacrificial dues. For the men who worked in the river, the Madan festival was a more important date than Onam, the traditional beginning of the new year.

The Vallamedu riverfront was approximately a square mile in area. During the monsoon, the river would rise and almost peep into the town of Vallam. The water would flow above the macadamized bridge, wetting one's ankles. The water would rush forth towards the sea that was barely a mile or two away. And the overflow would drain quickly once there was a let-up in the downpour and the rain persisted mildly. Vallamedu was a low plain and a confluence of two rivers. The water had deep inner currents and formed powerful eddies. Boatmen would not ply their vessels till the rains stopped completely and the flood subsided fully. There was one reason for their wait. It was only when the water level dropped that the sand fetched by the river from afar would settle and pile up.

Three

For the past several years, Angusami had been the sand contractor's star employee. Angusami was past his prime, but was a strong and energetic man. He knew every bend and curve of the river. He could row a boat, dip into the river and scoop up sand, and shovel the sand into neat heaps. He could get men to work well and check the boat to see if it needed repairs. He knew the heart and mind of the contractor and conducted the business to his satisfaction. His dealings were clean and he had earned a good name for himself. Among the crowd at the riverfront, Angusami, Damodaran and Panki stood out like the mud brought down by the river water. The latter two worked on the boat used for dredging sand. Damodaran was an employee the contractor valued. He was young and spirited, with a fine sense of humour, but circumspect too. He had come to Vallamedu from Tiruvitamkur at a young age and had no one to call his own. Angusami trusted him implicitly. Damodaran lived in a small room with a sloping roof at the back of Angusami's house and was regarded as a family member. Panki, a young woman, was the object of everyone's pity. Though strong in body, she was ugly to the point of being revolting, with her protruding eyes, flat nose and cleft lip. Her teeth were large, and her hands and legs were bleached because she constantly worked in the water. Panki was born to Angusami's wife, now no more. Panki was a burden that tormented Angusami, the darkest shadow of his life...

Angusami, Damodaran, Panki, the cart men, the riverfront god Madan Sami, and the flowing river – these were the pictures that filled the day's canvas...

Four

The light of dawn cracked the sky open. There blew a cool breeze, typical of the month of Aavani, after the rains ceased. Angusami was making his way to the river from the left incline of the bridge. He had covered himself with a towel to ward off the chill. He held the green sheath that he had peeled off a coconut palm on the way. Once he reached the bank, he took a look at his 'factory', now securely locked. Standing in ankle-deep water, he rinsed his mouth. The boats lay scattered all across the river. Someone was plying an empty boat eastwards. 'Who is this, going alone even before the sun is out?' he wondered aloud and tried hard to make out who it might be, but failed. 'Well, he must be a greedy fellow who wants to grab all the sand... Well, even if a river is in spate, a dog can only lick the water... Let him be... If I could make out who he is, I could give him a yelling. My eyes are not as sharp as they used to be...' he muttered to himself. He was irked, and finished cleaning his teeth with rude noises.

Angusami wiped his face and limbs with the towel. He

approached the idol of Madan and stood facing the east. He folded his hands and offered a prayer to the sun and the idol for a few moments, before walking to the shed.

The sun was rising. A pleasant fragrance wafted in with the breeze from the grove on the bank. Angusami drew out a dirty notebook from the niche and sat down on a stool. 'Good god, I have to be ready by eleven with two lorry-loads for the buyer from Vejnaramudu. This Panki... and Damodaran... I had told them to bring the men early and they are not here yet.' Restless, he gazed at that point of the bridge where they stepped down and crossed over.

'Is that Angusami Mooppan, so early? Salaam to you.' Meera Sahib, the boatman, came up to him. He was thin, had a grey moustache, and held a pole and an oar on his shoulder.

'Salaam Sahib, you call this early? Is it past seven or not? Well, you are here already and you are no young man. And look at these youngsters... they are still not here...'

'You mean your daughter and Damodaran? They are on the way. Why do you hurry so much? Let the chill lessen a bit. We are human, after all. One does hesitate to take a dip into cold water.'

'Since how many years have you and I been working in the river? Have you forgotten that we trowelled sand in the middle of the night and plied boats? Is it colder now than earlier? It is not impossible if there is a passion for work in your heart...'

'Look here, brother, forget about the past. Times have changed. Young men are not like they used to be. Keep that in mind. Now there's your daughter and your workers. I am going to take the boat across the river to bring coconut fibre for contractor Vasu, not to trowel sand. That's good business these days. Let me take my leave.' Meera Sahib stepped into the river and waded in the waist-deep water towards his boat.

Panki was coming down the path, followed by Damodaran, who was dressed in a vest and a lungi that was tied tight around his waist. He came into the shed, ready to plunge into work immediately, with a few men and women in tow. They carried crowbars, shovels and baskets. 'Wretch! Must drink tea to the gills and now strolls in at a snail's pace... Hurry up. There's plenty to do!' Angusami snapped venomously at Panki.

'Father's tongue is already coated with ginger,' said Panki to Damodaran in a low voice.

'Don't moan and mutter. The day is not far when I shall trample on your bones and crack each one of them, you wretch...'

'Anna, do we work or do we stand and hear you spewing out venom?' asked Damodaran.

'I didn't say anything to you, Damodaran, nothing at all. When I see this creature, some sort of lava wells up inside me. I say things that I am not even aware of...'

'You need no special cause to shout at her, we all know that... So, this morning do we go to Melakkuzhi? How many boatloads do we need?'

'Whether you go there or to Palattadi, near the Pala tree, we need two lorryfuls, by ten-thirty in the morning. I took an advance a week ago. Hurry up.'

Damodaran went out to the boats with Panki and the rest.

Five

'As a man grows older, his wisdom wanes. Don't you agree with me, Damodara Anna?'

'Why this thought, all of a sudden?'

'Well, I was thinking of father.'

'So it is only now that you think of his nature... I have known about him since I was this high... Panki, he is excessively worried about you. That's why he is more short-tempered than ever before.'

'Why this concern, all of a sudden? All told, my limbs are healthy and strong. I can hold a good load of sand. I haven't caused him any financial loss. This father of mine hates the sight of me. Because of this, he blabs to everyone that I am not fit for marriage. How fair is that? Am I insisting that I should be married off? I beg of you, Damodara Anna, tell father... that I am not going to become anyone's wife. Don't think that I'm saying this because my lack of beauty depresses me. I do not know why, but I despise the thought of marriage.'

'Panki, my girl, what's all this talk about? And all this to

Damodaran, who may one day marry you,' said one of the workers, laughing, as he dumped the sand onto the boat.

'Let's not talk about Damodara Anna deciding in my favour. Annan will marry a girl who is beautiful, in good health and has a good heart. Well, what is decreed will happen. Anyway, I want to see Anna getting married...Anna, why are you so quiet?'

'Well, what can I say when the two of you are prattling so much! I have no time for this silly talk. Your father would be standing on the bank, waiting. And the sun is already up. Shovel up, fast. The boat is not even half full. Or hand me that shovel. I'll show you how it's done,' said Damodaran, taking off his lungi and placing it on the prow of the boat. He jumped into the water in his shorts, quickly shovelled the sand into baskets and handed them over to Panki, who stopped talking and got busy working. Work continued apace and everyone was quiet.

'God, our hands and feet are stiff...we are going for our beedi...Panki, you should take a break too. Damodara, do you want a beedi?' Without waiting for a response, two workers picked up their lungis from the boat and walked to the shore.

Damodaran got into the boat, wiped his body and looked at Panki, who was wading in the water, apparently unaware of his presence. She scooped out a handful of water close to the prow, put it into her mouth and spat it out gently. 'Pankiyamma, you were lecturing us quite a bit a while ago. But there is not even a whisper from you now. Are you contemplating leading the life of an ascetic and remaining unmarried?'

Panki turned her face towards him. Her big eyes glistened,

coated by a film of tears.

'Panki, whatever has come over you today? What have I said to hurt you? Wipe your eyes. Or people will see it as a cause for their amusement.'

'Let people see, I do not care at all. It is true that no one is happy about having to look at me. I know that very well. I don't even have a dog for a friend. I had a mother and she is gone. Now no one needs me. I am asking you honestly, Damodara Anna, in the presence of the river, what's the need for me to live? I shall one day jump into it and give up my life.'

'No, no... You are hardly twenty and what kind of talk is that? Just a while ago, you said that you were strong of limb and that will earn you a living. And now you are willing to jump into the river... Panki, don't say things so thoughtlessly. Don't think so low about yourself. And even if your father, or anyone for that matter, hates you, this Damodara Annan is not going to do the same.'

Panki was moved when Damodaran uttered the word 'Annan'; sobs erupted from within.

'Now shut up, girl. Wipe your eyes. Those men are back. Shovel up that pile there as soon as the water has seeped down. As soon as they are here, you have to move the sand from the boat and go to the next one. Quick, wipe your face.'

The day became warmer. The sun beat down harshly on their backs, though it was not noon yet.

Two workers brought the boat to the shore, dumped the sand on the bank and returned to work in the river. From the thatched shed, Angusami gesticulated and yelled in the workers' language that the work be speeded up. The workers returned the call, conveying that they were indeed speeding up the work. As the sun rose higher and higher, the people's activity in the river grew more and more hectic. Boats crossed from one bank to the other continuously, now loaded with coils of rope, now empty. Or they carried men and women to and fro.

Under the shade of a tree, a couple of men were busy rubbing grease on a boat turned upside down. The cart drivers had freed the animals from their yokes. They wanted the boys to speed up the job of measuring the sand. 'We cannot wait here forever. Measure our load fast. We have other work to do.'

'If we speed it up, what you'll get is water, not sand. When you measure it at your end, it will weigh five instead of ten measures. Now shall I measure it out fast?'

'Well, you've got the money already, so you can talk the way you like.'

'It's because I have your money that I want to give you sand, and not water. Don't hurry us up, that's all I say. Listen, my man, the sand is not like a crop for which we sow seeds and reap a harvest. God gives it to us along with flood waters. We bend our backs and shovel it up. If we give it to you wet with water, we will have to answer Him.'

'We said nothing now for which we'll have to face divine retribution. Let's get going fast, for you have got the full payment, and that's all we said.'

'What's this war of words all about? Hold your peace, the two of you! The cart can move only after the sand is loaded, right? Hold it now,' an old man intervened, in an attempt to bring the heated exchange to an end. A piercing sound issued from the middle of the river, like an eagle's screech, a sound of distress. Men rushed to the bank and pedestrians crossing the bridge halted in their tracks.

Damodaran was plying the boat quickly towards the bank. The other workers crowded inside the boat were eagerly watching the shore come closer and closer.

'It is Panki. Yes, Panki fainted, wherever she was standing ... Luckily, Damodaran was standing next to her, so she escaped falling into the water,' shouted one of the workers as the boat approached the shore.

'Where is Angusami Mooppan? Isn't it his daughter who fainted?' asked someone.

Panki was made to lean on the pile of sand. Damodaran and a couple of other workers brought her to the bank, holding her to give her support. They laid her down on a woven mat inside the shed.

'Angusami Mooppan, you are here? You do not know what happened? This girl has fainted like this earlier too. Take her to a good doctor. After all, she is a young woman. You haven't bothered to get her married off and remain indifferent... You are the least bothered that so many men have gathered here...' said someone from the crowd.

Damodaran looked pointedly at Angusami. The latter stared at the river with a blank look on his face.

'Who's that? This is no party for everyone to be staring and talking about it. Keep away, don't crowd around her. Let her get some breeze. Appukutta, go and get a soda... She will soon be all right.'

Six

'Damodara, all that you say is true, I accept it. When her mother, Tangammai, was alive, what ties did I have with this girl? I didn't even think that such a creature existed in my house. That was probably Tangammai's fault. So what can be done about that? When Tangammai came into my life, I never found this one a hindrance. Tangammai left this world, as though she had suddenly had enough of it. And this girl is no baby. She should take care of herself. And she knows how to. I see so many women working in the river... Panki, for me, is just one of them. Yes, she cooks my rice gruel and vegetables and occupies a corner of the house. But I am certainly not going to pretend to cherish her like a daughter, this twit of a girl...I cannot force myself. I have lived my life in a respectable manner with her mother and have always had my norms...'

'Wait. Allow me to say one thing. Is Anna trying to tell me that this girl is behaving in an unbecoming manner?'

'It is clear that you just don't understand me. Tell me, in

what way is this girl connected to me?'

'If you ask me that, I have to ask you how Tangammai was related to you.'

'Agreed. Yes, she was my wife. But is there a law that I should accept a daughter that she begot from a stranger?'

'Don't seek the law in your support. Had Tangammai been alive, this question wouldn't have cropped up. But she's gone. And we are men with some responsibility and feeling of justice. The girl is grown up. By god's grace, she is a hard worker. She has caused no loss of any kind. It is your duty to get her married, at least for the sake of her mother's memory. Suppose you and Tangammai had borne a daughter like Panki, would you have pushed her into the river? So, treat her as your own till you entrust her to a safe pair of hands. Stop this display of hatred and anger. I can say for sure that her spells of giddiness are the result of your ill feeling towards her.'

'If she feels giddy or faints, it must be a birth defect. I have seen that throughout those ten or more years I spent with her mother, to whom I was attached like nail is to flesh. Still, I wasn't destined to see the face of my own offspring. And I tried everything I could, from medicine to magic. But none of it was bound to bear fruit, for this accursed creature was residing in my house. How could a new life germinate in her womb? An astrologer even said this in so many words. But I did not have faith in him…As you said, she is a strong-limbed girl. She can earn a living. Let her go away with some man. Let her mind her own life. I have no objection…'

'You are in the position of her father and you are a respectable man. Then why should she go away with someone? That is not defensible at all…'

'Damodara, leave me alone now. I see you as a son, so I heard you out. I decide what is just and what is not just for me. So far, I haven't succumbed to anyone. Go now. We can talk later.'

Damodaran took leave of Angusami. He knew well that Angusami resisted being influenced by anybody.

Seven

After two days of extreme fatigue, Panki, who was on her feet once again, felt that everything around was drained of the sap of life. The breeze blew as usual, but the movement of the leaves on the trees was perfunctory, she thought.

The pumpkin vine creeping over the roof of the shed in the backyard was full of blooms that resembled yellow umbrellas. Panki dumped the left-over kitchen ash at the base of the stem of a yam plant. Each of those stems was as thick as a forearm and had a profusion of spots, like those of a snake, and each leaf on the short stem was a shady umbrella...

A terrible stench emanated from the pot in which she collected water to wash rice. For the last two days, she had not visited the adjacent cattle shed to pour water for the cows. Nor had she collected cowdung, so essential for cleaning the kitchen. The house had turned into a mess in two days. Panki began to put things in order, one by one. Angusami had left for the riverfront early in the morning. The room where he slept was strewn with beedi-ends and matchsticks.

She swept out the beedi-ends and matchsticks, and folded all his clothes and hung them neatly on the clothesline. She needed to fetch water from the common well to scrub and wash the dirty utensils. The mud pot was coated with moss. She threw the stale water near the banana tree and walked to the well.

'Panki, is that you? I heard that you were not well. I had no time to come and see you, thanks to my son's father...he causes a commotion if I am not there even for a moment.'

This was the neighbour, a woman who was not too young and who spoke unceasingly of 'her son's father', who took her to every film that was showing in town and who always bought her something special from the shop. 'And if I have even so much as a headache, my son's father acts like a man who has become delirious. He'll be sprinting to the doctor's, heating water...somewhat like a small-scale Puram festival.' To lend substance to her pretence of concern for Panki, she added, 'Come here, girl. Your hair is such a mess.' She ran her fingers through her hair, took out a couple of lice and duly punctured them on her thumbnail with noises of disgust. 'Your head is full of lice. If you come to my house every now and then, I can at least comb your hair and tie it up. Poor girl. If you keep carrying baskets on your head, you will be left with only a balding patch on top. If one is motherless, the father is just a distant uncle. And for you, he is in fact that in reality. Your day breaks on the face of the river. When the sun sets you have to cook for that father of yours. Panki, I heard that your father doesn't even talk to you. When you were ill, did he take even a cursory interest? But for Damodaran, that good boy, you would have had a bad time.'

'Akka, why do you drag in Damodaran? He is an outsider,

all said and done. What's more, this poor creature is too plain to set tongues wagging,' added a third woman, who had just arrived at the well. She derived a sense of satisfaction out of having managed to slip in that Panki could never be alluring to men.

'I have lots of work to do, Akka,' said Panki, quickly throwing the bucket into the well. She had no desire to fill more than a single pot. Her mind was blank as she sat down in front of the house. A pregnant black bitch with swollen teats came running up to her and stretched herself at her feet.

Panki was unaware of the passage of time. As evening began to darken in slow stages, Damodaran came up the path leading to the house. Panki was lost to the world. The bitch slunk off as he approached Panki. He had to call out her name more than once to startle her into her senses.

'Has Anna been here for long?'

'Now, Panki, what's all this? You are not even aware that someone is inside the house. It is evening and you haven't lit the lamp. Light the lamp. Mooppan had stepped into the river for a wash when I left. He'll eat something at the hotel and come home. Here, here's some food in this packet. You didn't cook anything, did you?... I thought as much... Put away the packet. I'll go and change.'

'Wait a little, Anna. I overheard what you and father said about me. If you have any affection for me, don't discuss me with him at all. I can take care of myself. And I have no desire to take my life. I, too, have thought about things... and I am certainly going to fight and hold my head high.'

Damodaran was pleased to hear the confident note in Panki's voice.

'Only now do I see the real Panki, who has spunk. You

should live, whatever the odds. If something untoward happens, it can be faced, whenever it happens. There is some puttu and fruit in that packet. Eat it. Light the lamp, pull up the wick for a bright light. Come with me to the river tomorrow in a good frame of mind. You don't feel ill now, do you? If the mind isn't tired, the body too doesn't feel tired. I cannot do my best when you are not on the boat. Today, we had Rajammai carrying the loads... She is quite a worker, this Rajammai...'

'Rajammai? Damodara Anna, yes, she is a good girl. Cast your noose around her. It will be useful.' Panki laughed aloud, in a carefree manner.

'There you are, with your favourite habit of teasing... Well, I am happy to see you laugh! Mooppan will be here any minute now. I shall see you later... I haven't washed yet.' Damodaran took leave of Panki.

Eight

Panki was full of fresh energy as she went for work after a gap of four days. There was less water in the river due to the onset of summer. Boats huddled in the middle of the river. The sky was a clear and bright blue, without a cloud. The sun was burning hot, except where the bridge cast a shadow on the river. Two elephants were being bathed in a part of the shallows. The boatmen enjoyed the sight of the animals spraying water on themselves with their trunks. Panki stepped into the water with empty baskets. One of the girls spoke to her in a loud voice.

'Ei, Panki! You haven't changed and you are rushing into the water…'

Panki changed into a checked lungi behind a tree. The crowd at the river was more cheerful than usual. She noticed that even Angusami was chatting with someone in a rather loud voice.

Damodaran and a few others were filling the baskets. The women, their heads covered with palmyra 'hats', carried the sand and dumped it on a boat used for harvesting sand. As Panki arrived, all of them enquired about her condition. 'I wanted so much to come and see you...and whenever I got ready, something or the other intervened and I postponed it for the next day,' said one.

'When we asked Mooppan for the directions to your house, he did not tell me. "Mind your own business, girl," he said. "She is just lying at home." He didn't show a trace of concern...'

'So you are busy sharing news? Let your mouths do the talking; the rest of you can work. Panki, come here with your basket...' Damodaran broke up their little meeting.

As work continued apace, somebody shouted from the spot where the elephants were being bathed. 'The elephant has slipped into a trough...Please come! Help!' The men and women threw their shovels and baskets into the boat and rushed to the spot, already crowded with people.

The female elephant had slipped and fallen into a trough that was full of slush. The trough had been formed because of the removal of sand from that spot. The animal's hind legs seemed to be caught inextricably in a wedge. The mahouts had put a rope around the necks of both elephants and were coaxing the male to tug the female out. As the male pulled, the female cried in pain, but could not move. The crowd on the bank swelled. All work came to a standstill.

Each person proposed a solution. The mahout said that someone had to get into the shallows and find out where the elephant's legs were stuck, and then pull out the animal accordingly. No one had the courage to dive so close to the elephant's feet. The sand workers, without exception, refused to oblige. A few wondered about the nature of the trough –

was it rocky or slushy, or was it moving sand?

'That spot has some slippery rocks. Why take the animals to those shallows when this place is as big as a sea?' asked Damodaran.

'We never led them to that spot. It was while stepping up towards the shore that the elephant slipped. How were we to know that the bottom is so uneven even in these floodless days?'

The male elephant was shedding tears as his companion struggled and strained to extricate her legs and move towards the bank.

'If we, who spend each day of our lives on the river, do not know what type of rock it is, it's a shame. A mute animal struggles for life and we watch it as though it is a festival. What a sense of justice!...Move away, you! I shall go in. You are the sorts who look for signs even on the surface of the water...' said Angusami. He tied up his veshti to enter the river.

'Damodara Anna, tell father not to go in. That elephant is in pain and can harm him. Why can't a younger man go?' said Panki.

'Annan need not go into the water. Let me see what it is...' said Damodaran. A few others joined him.

'We aren't letting anyone go in alone near the elephant's feet. Angusami Anna should stay on the shore. The river is like the mother who bore us. We should no longer wait and watch the suffering of a mute animal. Step into the trough. You, mahout, we are getting in for better or for worse. Keep watching the elephant.'

The crowd was now close to the edge of the water. Angusami stood in knee-deep water, at a distance. The crowd praised him. But for him, they said, none of the younger people would have taken up the challenge. The frightened elephant, doubly assailed by the shouting and milling crowd, trumpeted furiously. The mahout dug in the goad repeatedly, mauling the poor creature. Seeing the animal's agitation, the men hesitated before plunging into the river.

The crowd yelled, in complete disregard of the fact that this would upset the beasts. Suddenly, the stricken elephant managed to release its legs and fell towards the bank. There was plenty of water where it fell and a huge spray descended on the crowd. The suddenness with which the elephant freed its legs and the ensuing spray of water made the crowd run pell-mell.

'Don't run, don't... nothing has happened to the elephant... Look, it has stood up and it is walking. If you are so unruly, it will get upset,' shouted the mahout.

By the time the crowd came to its senses and the elephant reached the bank with its bleeding feet, something else had happened.

Angusami too had scampered on to the bank in the melee, but had slipped and fallen into the water. Damodaran and the other workers took him to the shed. 'I seem to have twisted my left arm, though I haven't hurt the rest of my body. I can't lower it, it's too painful. Get a cart ready for me. The pain is too severe.'

Panki and the others were surprised that Angusami should show such obvious distress.

'Father should be immediately taken to a bone doctor... He cannot take the pain,' said Panki.

Damodaran quickly took charge. The cart was soon ready to take Angusami to the doctor.

When the wounded elephant and the mahout left, the place looked forlorn, like a deserted market. The river, its waters lean since the arrival of summer, flowed serenely, as though nothing had happened on its bank.

Nine

Nothing really affects the world. Morning dawns every day, like all other days. It turns into day and then the sun sets. Night arrives, and then the day dawns.

When we observe the human species as a whole, there is nothing much that is worth mentioning. Everyone is busy with their responsibilities. Everybody eats. Everybody seeks joy. Everybody sleeps. Within this order, in a remote corner, there exist the sick, the starving and the maimed paupers. Amid the bustle of the world's movement, pain and suffering are of little consequence. Both flux and quiet coexist on the stage of the world... Isn't it pointless to light a lamp inside a pot to dispel darkness?

Angusami's dislocated arm seemed to be a simple affair at first. But healing it was no simple matter. The upper arm bone had come out of the shoulder joint. When the bone doctor set it by stepping on it, the pain was excruciating and Angusami imagined that death was at hand. His debility grew worse day by day and he remained confined to bed. The arm could not be aligned with the body and the shoulder was swollen. There was a constant nagging pain. The doctor came every morning and massaged every muscle and sinew with oil. 'Does it hurt here? It cannot be hurting here… Is this too bad?' He pressed every inch of his arm with his finger.

'It is the shoulder that feels terrible. And the side. Doctor, I am not one to exaggerate ordinary aches. This one is boring a hole into my chest, it is so terrible. I got into that melee just to help a mute animal…and that has landed me in this condition. This pain should stop. I wouldn't mind it if I had to lose the use of this arm…' said Angusami. His obvious distress affected Panki and Damodaran deeply.

'Angusami, don't get depressed. Your bone was dislocated from the clavicle. It has been put back in place. Now, this oil should be rubbed on the spot every day. Once the swelling comes down, it will be fine. Yours is not a young body, after all. So it will take time to heal. In the evening, you should apply a paste of freshly ground mimosa, salt and sweet lime, after heating it. Pankiyamma, you should do this diligently. Don't worry, I shall see you later.' The doctor gave them the necessary medicines, comforted Angusami and left.

It was the fourth day since Angusami had been laid up in bed. Panki stayed at home. Damodaran visited them every evening, got the provisions they needed and escorted the doctor to their house.

'Father has been feeling better since yesterday. I'll cook his gruel and vegetables and go for work tomorrow,' said Panki.

'What's the hurry? You can postpone that by two more days,' said Damodaran.

'Damodara,' Angusami called out from the room in which

he was lying. Damodaran and Panki were standing in the passage, wondering why he had called.

'Damodara!'

'Yes, what is it?'

'Panki need not stay back. Let her go to the river. It is only my arm that has to improve. If the doctor had not forbidden me to walk, I would have gone and sat down in the shed. I feel as though I am chained. Lying down all the while. This is my fate. Why drag her into it? Let her go to work tomorrow,' said Angusami.

Ten

Everything seemed empty to Angusami. Panki went out to work. It seemed as though he had lain in bed for aeons.

There was nothing that he looked forward to. He could do nothing. How long he was destined to lie down and depend on Panki he could not tell. Death was indeed a deliverer from all sorts of worries. Had Tangammai been alive, he would have felt greatly consoled. Now he had nobody to call his own. He was alone, like a river at night. A total loner.

But if he went back as far as his memory took him, had he not always been a solitary person? Why this thought, now? As a stronger man full of verve and vim, he had not bothered about anyone. For the first time in his life, he was incapacitated... but surely, this was not the end! He would be fine in a fortnight. It was just a brief illness... Such cowardice – for a man to think of his last days and ruminate over his end! Once he recovered, he would have to repay that girl in some manner and be up and about, as always.

The doctor was giving him a medicine. It was bitter. It

was utter idiocy to withdraw oneself...No, enough of this listlessness...

A breeze was blowing outside. The branches of the trees swayed. It felt a bit cold. But he felt averse to pulling up the blanket with one hand...He looked at the door with its criss-cross of blackened reeds, which gave the impression of short skeletal bones. The woven fibre that used to fill them had given way. The thatch had not been redone for a number of years. It ought to be done before the rains arrived. And just like redoing the thatch, everything had to be looked into anew. Life had to be lived again. A new beginning had to be made. The walls too had not received a coating for a long time. During the monsoon, the roof had started leaking and, in turn, brown streaks had dripped down the mud walls, appearing now like dry scars.

As long as Tangammai was alive, their lives were marked by economy and a sense of order. He had not had a haircut for months now. His face looked terrible, with a few days growth of stubble. There was a small mirror on the wall. The dirty brown shirt and veshti hung on the clothesline in a corner. A black trunk stood in the other corner, like a baby elephant. Beedis, a matchbox, a smoke-filled hurricane lamp and old copies of the magazine, *Malayala Manorama*, lay on top of the trunk. The bottle containing the oil prescribed by the doctor was still full. The room reeked of medicine.

Well, how long could he keep lying down? Angusami held his hurt arm aloft and opened the single window that faced the south. The midday sun shone like gold. The short green stems of the cassava plant (from which tapioca is extracted) had a cooling effect on the eye. Beyond was the single room that Damodaran occupied. The thatch looked grey with age.

The room would be locked. That was where he too had begun his life... Would Damodaran work hard, strive like he had? Would he marry... Panki? Like he had married Tangammai? Now, what sort of useless thought was that? Panki was as ugly as Damodaran was good-looking, and never could the two be a couple. This creature was lucky to be receiving his brotherly regard. He was a good fellow, without a doubt. How did he happen to enter his life?... He was a mere boy and Tangammai was still alive...

So much had changed, but Damodaran had not. He was loyal, steadfast... That was surprising, considering the times one lived in...

Smiling face, dark body, of medium height. He never spoke in a loud voice. He was so sympathetic towards Panki, who, as a rule, evoked revulsion in anyone who set his or her eyes on her. A good man, with a good heart. The river was his playground and the boat, his mount. The beloved son of the river, into which he plunged every day to shovel sand; which he crossed in his boat by holding the pole firm against the riverbed, even when a powerful current countered his efforts. He was the river's favourite son, its adopted son, growing up in its lap. The river was his life. He was as cool and full. The deep affection evoked by his thoughts about Damodaran brought tears to Angusami's eyes.

It was not possible to stand at the window any longer. He felt weak after just four days of illness. And that ignoble creature with a body so perishable puts up such an exaggerated show of self-worth, he told himself.

Eleven

Angusami went back to the cot and lay down. He then noticed that Panki had left a brew of coffee and jaggery for him in an aluminium mug, covered with a plate, on top of the trunk. He did not feel like getting up again to pick up the mug and drink the coffee.

Panki! That ugly face floated before him like a big disc.

'Appan, don't drink plain cold water when you are thirsty. I have left some coffee brew in a mug.' After she had said this, with that face and that nose – so ugly, like a ball, starting immediately beneath her eyebrows – and those close eyes, he could not feel thirsty at all. Tangammai was dark, but she was so beautiful and so perfect. Panki could never be presented before the world as his ward... Her body was strong and firm, like a plump statue of Kali. Otherwise, even dogs would have barked at the sight of her.

He thought of the girls who worked on the riverfront – Pulachi, Maalai, Tandathi and Ammu, the coolies, Chellamma and Bhanu, the helpers, and Bhavani, Rajamma and Bayi, the ezhava girls...He recalled their faces, their dirty, wet clothes and the way they worked. And in their midst worked this creature, who was ugliness unredeemed, irredeemable...

'There, that ugly girl, who is it?' a new buyer or lorry driver would blurt out on seeing her for the first time, unable to bear the assault of her ugliness on his senses.

'Don't you know, she is Angusami Mooppan's daughter?'

'No, it cannot be...'

'Hard to believe...? It is his wife's daughter.'

'Say that. She doesn't even remotely look like Mooppan. So she's not his own daughter, thank god...'

When he heard such talk, he felt a sense of relief that people readily believed that she was not his daughter. Even this meagre consolation was reduced to dust when she stood before him and said, 'Appa, your gruel is ready.' Just who was she, calling him her father? A feeling of disgust welled up in him and he was ready to scream at her lest she hover into his view.

Damodaran often said to him, 'Anna is habitually bad-mouthing the girl.'

Angusami lay like a nearly unconscious person within a froth of bitter thoughts about Panki.

'Mooppare, Mooppare...' Angusami opened his eyes when he heard someone addressing him. It was Meera Sahib, the boatman, with his tall frame and prominent grey moustache.

'Sahib? Come in, sit down. There, on that box. Spread that paper.'

'Don't get so flustered. Here, I have sat down comfortably. I was not here all these days. Someone related to me had a baby and I went to Pottankadu to see her. Yesterday I went to the river to ply my boat and heard the news. Should you have got into the water? I heard that you slipped and fell. We have seen so much of this water – flood and slush – and still such a thing happens. Well, that's destiny, unavoidable, be it good or bad. We mussalmans call it "musibat"... Was it a bad hit?'

'Good or bad I cannot tell. I have to suffer for some days... See, I cannot move this arm. There is a swelling in the joint above the arm. The bone doctor visits me every day and massages it with oil... He says that it will take time to heal since I am not so young... Here, look...'

'Mooppare, don't try to get up. Just lie down. Since you are unable to move your arm, you should have told your daughter to stay at home for a few days and take care of you, and not work in the river.'

'Sahib, I am not such a rich man. How long can one stay away from work? And you say that she's my daughter... how is that right? Have you thought of that?'

'When I ask you about that girl, you begin to talk like a madman...'

'Yes, I am mad. Talk about something else. Did you go to the pier today? What is the price of sand?'

'Sand? Who wants sand and mud in the month of Kanni? No one wants to buy it even if it is five paise per bushel. It is five days since I pushed my boat into the river. A few boys are still shovelling sand. Your daughter is working at the brick kiln, carrying loads...'

'What of Damodaran?'

'The girl followed him... He is working at the kiln. Why not marry the girl to Damodaran? There are many young people on the riverfront – men and women – but he always seeks her out, talks to her and jokes with her. I think he might even marry her...'

'Sahib! He is a number one fellow. The two have grown up together since they were children. Thanks to me, we have such mutual concern though he lives separately. He is certainly not attracted by this "beauty". He is bound to marry a suitable woman sooner or later.'

'It seems you wouldn't let him marry her even if he wished to...'

'No, I shall not agree. I will not allow a young and deserving man to marry this defaced creature. I'll drown this half-creature in the river, but won't permit Damodaran to marry her... He matters to me, not she.'

'Mooppare, you may deny it with all your might, but she is your daughter by custom. Why does your heart turn so dry when it comes to anything that concerns her? You are not a heartless sort. Or a callous type. Why does your heart become so dry when it comes to her?'

'Why does our heart turn so dry?' The question reverberated in his ears like a wail, echoing loud and long.

Twelve

The gruelling sun became milder as the day progressed. Angusami lay in bed, hovering between sleep and wakefulness. Bitter thoughts about Panki lingered in his mind, like oil on water...

A breeze was blowing outside. So much time had flown away... with the wind.

❖

A yellow light slanted down from the sky. As the light hit the rich green, tongue-shaped leaves of the tapioca, its colour changed and took on a silvery tinge. The thick tamarind trees stood tall and there was a small thatched house close by. A small veranda washed with cow dung and water, an inner room, a store. If one stepped down from the back, the kitchen was to the left. From the kitchen, a thatched door opened out into a sizeable and fragrant grove, full of manjanatti trees, pear trees with their ash-coloured bark that glistened like great snakes, and ilava trees, which sent up branches like upright crosses. The grove was enclosed by a nine-foot-high wall of black stone. On the other side of the wall was an open ground that housed the police training school, made of red earth, and the administrative office, a yellow building. And adjacent to the wall was a small temple with a tiled roof, dedicated to Hanuman. This was the god favoured by the policemen.

Tangammai lived in that house under the tamarind trees. She was dark, yes, but beautiful! Her appearance did not betray that she was the mother of a child. She was the daughter of Kuttan Mestiri, who cooked for the police camp. Angusami was a coolie in the marketplace, two miles away from the pier. He had left his native town, Thoothukudi, at a young age to pull carts here. He used to rest in squalid corners and shopfronts. He was now a strong and straight-backed young man, capable of earning a steady income. He was unlike other young men, who did not mind frittering away their time and money and leading unsettled lives. Though he was no more than a coolie, he wished to live with dignity, have a decent hearth and home and enjoy the fruits of leaving home for a new place. These considerations prompted him to rent a small thatched hut that happened to be close to Tangammai's house.

When he took a look at the hut, he found that it was full of dirt. However, he had not brought anything along to clean the place with. He then caught sight of the house above. He went there immediately and it was then that he set eyes on Tangammai for the first time.

'Who are you? What do you want?' she said, coming out of the house. She was wearing a checked kaili and a white blouse. The topmost fold had been tucked into the blouse. Angusami was by nature a shy man and preferred to avoid encounters with women. The sudden confrontation with womanhood in its prime threw him off balance and he cast his eyes down momentarily. He got a grip on himself and spoke.

'I have taken the thatched hut below your house on rent. I didn't bring anything to clean the place with. If I might borrow a broom…'

'I live here with my father and my child. My father is a cook in the police camp. You may be knowing Kuttan Mestiri…'

'Oh, don't I know him! It is due to his kindness that I got this hut on rent. But I did not know that Kuttan Mestiri had a daughter.'

'If you have got it because of him, you must be an honourable man,' she said with a smile.

Angusami was unnerved by such straightforward talk. Composing himself a second time, he asked for a broom.

'Who is going to sweep?' said Tangammai.

'Why bring a person along especially for that? I can do all sorts of work,' said Angusami with a little more confidence now.

'You are not like other men, I'd say. If I delay any further, you might come in and take it yourself! I'd be the least surprised…!' she laughed and handed him the broom.

From that moment on, Tangammai's smiling face was framed in Angusami's heart.

Every day he would leave early in the morning and come home at eight or nine, when day had turned into night. He would be so tired after the day's work that all he could think of was stretching his body and going off to sleep, without even a stray thought of the world around him. A single room, a grass mat, a pillow, a mud pitcher to hold water, an aluminium tumbler, an iron bucket, a tin of charred rice chaff that he used as a tooth scrub, a small mirror, a stool that had cost him three-and-a-half rupees, a broom in the corner – these were his belongings.

On the last Thursday of each month, bhajans could be heard from the Hanuman temple in the police camp. By the time he got around to contemplating how god put up with that raucous chorus issuing from the throats of the policemen, he would succumb to sleep.

One Thursday, however, Angusami happened to remain awake for a long time as the cacophony went on. He had carried sacks of salt, a whole truckload of them. He had scrubbed himself and washed at the tap in the corner of Samiyar hotel. But his back felt itchy. He tossed from side to side, unable to sleep. An owl hooted in the dark from somewhere within the tamarind trees. The crickets seemed to do a better job, sounding like innumerable tiny anklet bells tinkling in unison. Every now and then, the police chorus abruptly intruded into the night sounds. He inured himself to the noises surrounding him and had nearly succeeded in drifting off to sleep.

Suddenly a piercing scream shook him up.

He woke up with a start and tried to guess the direction from which the sound had come. Before he could do this, he heard it again. It was a female voice from the house above. Without waiting further, he ran towards Kuttan Mestiri's house.

Kuttan Mestiri was walking back and forth in front of the house. He saw Angusami in the dim glow of the hurricane lamp.

'Is that the new tenant?... It's nothing. You must have

been frightened by my daughter's screams. I did expect that you'd get scared by the sound... It is nothing really. Whenever they have a special puja in the Hanuman temple, she gets possessed... She screams twice and swoons, falling like a branch that has been lopped off. That's all... You can see her, lying there. She isn't aware of anything.'

From the threshold, he could see Tangammai lying on the bare floor. She gave the impression of a policeman standing at attention, her limbs stiff and straight. The swell of her bosom and her face looked beautiful. Was she the one who had screamed? No, that was hard to believe... Even as this thought took shape in his mind, he saw that five-year-old – Panki – in the dull light. Was that a human child? Looked more like an owlet. Huge eyes, runny nose, frothing mouth, rough and bristly hair... That ugly apparition almost prevented the image of beauty from captivating his mind.

'Young man, sit down. This is nothing to be afraid of. This is caused by Hanuman's spirit. She is still under that influence. Now she will go to sleep and day will dawn as usual... I wanted to visit you in your house, but I didn't get the time... A policeman used to live there. He got married and left. This compound, with its trees, belongs to the government. It is ours as long as we are here. This rental is in confidence. The grove is like a forest and is not ours... I did go to look you up in the evening, but your door was closed.'

'I work in the marketplace. I have to work from dawn to night. Even the birds are back in their nests at sunset, but we superior creatures might return well past evening, even midnight. After which we bathe and sleep...'

'Brother, are you from Nagarcoil or Pandiya Nadu?'

'I come from Thoothukudi, from Xavier Street. But now

I belong to the market and the townsfolk here. I left home at a very young age, in a fit of anger. I am close to thirty now. I neither plan to return, nor did anyone come looking for me. Now how is it that you speak such good Tamil?'

'My profession is that of a cook. And I meet policemen who are on transfer here from other places. They also take me to their camps, to other camps. I know Tamil, I can also speak some Hindi and English.'

'Permit me to take my leave. I must sleep,' said Angusami. Mestiri accompanied him to the door.

'Go and sleep without any fear.'

'Fear? Why should I be afraid?'

'Yes, I realize that you are not a man given to fear . . . By the way, why shouldn't you marry and settle down?'

'I have no such desire.'

'Well, that is in keeping with the spirit of the bachelor god in the temple nearby. Isn't that funny? Well, go and sleep. We won't talk any more, in the dark.'

Angusami returned to his room.

Thirteen

The next morning, when he went out to clean his teeth, he cast a look at Mestiri's house. His eyes fell on that ugly creature and he wanted to throw up. As he cleaned his teeth, he spat out the contents of his mouth in her direction, more violently than he need have. Perhaps because of that noise, Tangammai stopped sweeping the entrance and peered in his direction.

'I got scared last night. Who was that stranger?' said Angusami with a smile.

Tangammai made no attempt to reply. Instead, she smiled shyly and drew random lines on the loose earth with her toe. In the east, the rising sun shone on the lush green treetops. Mynahs, sparrows and bulbuls trilled a sweet-throated medley of songs honouring the arrival of a new day. A blackbird with a long tail sat on the leafless silk cotton tree and struck a rhythm with its beak. Though Angusami had been there for some time, it was only now that he experienced the thrill of the morning hour.

'If the spirit of Hanuman is to arrive at night, he should inform us. There are some things I want to know that I'd like to ask that god,' said Angusami.

'Don't insult Hanuman. It is only when god deems it fit that one knows what one seeks.'

'I did not mean to insult your god. When he visits again, I too shall seek something. That's all I meant.'

'You can. I thought you were a simple person since you look as timid as a cat. But you are not timid at all, I see.'

'Well, even I had thought so. It's only after I heard that sound that I realized that you are no cat.'

'Ammachi, Grandpa is calling you,' said the creature, pulling at Tangammai's clothes. Tangammai smiled at Angusami and went into the house. The creature contorted its face to show its displeasure with him. 'Get out of my sight, wretch!' muttered Angusami under his breath. He finished cleaning his teeth and turned back.

If that apparition had not dragged her mother away at the behest of her grandfather, he could have had a more interesting talk with Tangammai. The thought kept gnawing at him...

His attraction for Tangammai and his hatred of Panki seemed to have germinated simultaneously.

❖

Angusami woke up with a start. The golden evening light was curving down the domed sky above the greenery outside the window. He felt very hungry as he had eaten nothing the whole day.

What to do now? Let Damodaran come back. And that ill-fated creature. Why did he always call her an ill-fated creature? He did eat what she cooked. He did accept her care. The very sight of her filled him with hatred, yes, but was there even a thing he could do without her? Damodaran was close to him, no doubt. Still, he was an outsider.

He could hear them talk as they arrived. Panki stepped in. Damodaran would come after changing in his room.

'Appa!' she called him softly.

He never responded to her as a rule.

As she entered, she saw Angusami stretched out on the cot. She thought he was asleep and took off the lid of the aluminium vessel. It was full, just as she had left it in the morning. 'Appa, are you sleeping?' she asked, turning to him. Angusami turned over on to his side and looked at her silently.

'I see father has not drunk anything. I shall cook some rice. Damodara Anna will be back right away.' She went into the kitchen.

'Father has stayed off food today. Won't he become weaker, especially when he has an injury? How will he gain the strength to get up? You Anna, you should tell him,' Panki told Damodaran, busying herself in the kitchen.

'Annan, you ate nothing. Isn't that childish?'

'Not that I didn't want to eat, Damodaran. Meera Sahib came today and we talked. We recalled the good old days and then I drifted off to sleep…When I opened my eyes, it was evening.'

'So there's nothing serious, thank god. Today, there was little work in the river. I and your daughter carried hot bricks at the kiln. And in the midst of this season of "plenty", plans are afoot to celebrate the sacrificial festival for Madan on the tenth of next month. Each person has to contribute two rupees.'

'Um... What else is new?'

'Till summer gets over, things are going to be lean.'

'And to top it all, I am laid up in bed. Did you see the doctor? Did he have anything to say?'

'But he did say yesterday that you will recover within a month, didn't he?'

'If I recover before that, it will be fine by me. I can't stay put like this any more, as though I am tethered...'

'How can Anna say such things?' protested Damodaran. 'Is there anyone in this world who does not fall ill? One should be patient, one should learn to tolerate...'

'Damodara!'

'Yes?'

'You know as well as me how much I have endured. Did this loner deserve all this? Tell me now.'

'Why is Anna so despondent, as though his boat has overturned? When Tangammai was alive, weren't you happy? There are pluses and minuses in whatever man does. God has given human beings the power to enjoy happiness when it comes their way. And one should bear it when there is unpleasantness...'

'Hey you! There is still some more time before you reach the age for preaching! But you will know it when you face it. Anyhow... Am I unhappy because I cannot enjoy things?'

'What could it be then? What is it that you must do, that bothers you so much? Just a small responsibility towards the girl, that's all. Come what may, as soon as you get well, you have to make sure that she is properly settled. Once you have done that, there is no burden on you at all.'

'This girl's future? Well, you can see for yourself how things are. Isn't this the only reason why I feel that I have swallowed fire?'

'If Damodara Annan accompanies him, father will eat at least a mouthful of rice. Food is ready,' said Panki, coming into the room.

Panki, the poor wretch, thought Damodaran. She had performed yet another task no sooner had she returned after a hard day's work, unmindful of the dead weight of Angusami's palpable hatred for her. True, her face put one off totally, whatever her good qualities. He thought he could understand Angusami, who had been bearing it for so long. Hers was an ugliness that was beyond redemption. It was as if this ugliness was a coborn of that negative emotion, hatred.

Fourteen

When one is ill and laid up in bed, one's mind also becomes as weak as one's body. The first thought that strikes a weakened mind is that of death. Let me die, thought Angusami. And if he did die, of what consequence was it to anyone? There was no one for him. Had he been rich and prosperous, there would have been a number of people flocking to him, claiming to have one relationship or the other with him.

His mind, he thought, was like low-lying land that was always wetter than the surrounding area. In the evening of his life it was thoughts of Tangammai that stayed – and springs that came to life – centrestage whenever his mind calmed down and became level.

❖

The groves stretched out ahead as far as one's eyes could see. Day had passed and the sun was about to set soon. The evening hours were beguiling on their side of the high stone wall bordering the grove. The policemen in khaki pants and white vests stood in a row, doing their exercises. All of them had perfect bodies and followed the leader's orders to stretch their arms and legs and jump.

In a corner of the grove, Tangammai was engrossed watching this disciplined drill, while at the same time, trying to contain the goat that she was grazing, for it was tugging hard to free itself from the tether.

Outside the wall, the front gate of the Hanuman temple was locked. On the side of the wall was painted, in vivid colours, a picture of the handsome god in his transcendental form, the viswarupa. Inside the grilled door the god stood tall. A big lump of butter lay on the plate of naivedya (offering). The fragrance of joss stick and jasmine emanated from the puja altar across the wall.

As Tangammai stood absorbed watching the policemen display their physical prowess, the goat suddenly took fright and tried to run in the opposite direction, bleating. The tugging of the animal brought her to her senses, and she dragged it closer, calmed it down and looked up. A shiny black cobra and a krait were entwined around each other and were fighting ferociously. Whenever the hold of one snake over the other slackened, it would tighten its grip with renewed vigour, try to swallow its adversary, beat its tail, turn, twist, roll and spin, like a whirling current of water, and fight on. The goat bleated in fright and tried to pull away. 'Stay still, you! It won't do anything...' she tried to tell the animal. Her hands had turned red and hurt with the effort of restraining the goat. She ran up the rough earth and suddenly saw a man looking at her from a rocky outcrop. It was Angusami!

'So, you are competing with a goat in a race!' he said in

a teasing tone. His arms were crossed over his chest and he stood blocking her way, like the Nandi bull. It was indeed a vantage point.

'Goodness, it's you! Back so early today? And surely, it is strange that you have come up here,' said Tangammai. Her face was red and she seemed flustered. She looked more beautiful than ever, and she felt shy for no apparent reason.

'Good that I came back early. Or you would have screamed like that night. That's clear from the way you look!' Angusami teased her.

'Look, I am not one to be frightened easily. There, in that corner, two snakes were fighting. The goat got scared and ran, fearing for its life... I couldn't stop it and had to follow it. That's why I'm sweating like this, like a wet mop.'

'Yes, yes, like they say: "I fell, but nothing happened." Don't pretend, I've been watching the scene for some time...'

'So, you've been back for a while?'

'Yes, I came back long ago, when those policemen were doing their exercises. The snake fight took place much later!'

'You are a good man, indeed! Why did you watch me secretly instead of calling out to me?'

'I could have. But I doubt that you would have heard me.'

'Indeed! But why?'

'When you were so absorbed watching that display of perfection... you would not hear me, I thought.'

Tangammai got a jolt. She shrank inwardly, as though her most intimate secret had come out before another person. Still, she regained her composure quickly.

'I was certainly not lost to the world! Well, yes, I was watching them. But what is there to get lost in? It's the same exercises that I've been seeing since childhood. The little one went off to sleep early, so I thought I'd take the goat to graze... I prayed to Hanuman. Then the exercises began... I do have to pass the time, right? Your implication that I was watching something just for fun is so typical of a man... You goat! Don't panic any more... Those snakes stopped fighting as soon as they heard human steps.'

They had both reached the front yard. The sounds accompanying the police exercises had receded into the background.

The jackfruit tree cast a large shadow before the entrance. Its rounded brown leaves had fallen on the ground. The young green leaves high up appeared golden in the setting sun. With its thick branches and abundant fruit, the tree was like an ageing, fecund woman. The fruits, big and small, were easy to reach and were obviously not sought after.

Tangammai tethered the goat and requested Angusami to come into the house. Angusami appeared reluctant to do so. 'I have work. I merely happened to walk this way from the road. I have to bathe... Let me go.' He seemed to be giving himself airs.

'You have come as far as the entrance. Nothing will go wrong if you sit here for a few minutes. Father will be coming a little late tonight. The IG is here and he has to cook special stuff... You may sit on this.' She quickly fetched a stool from inside.

'No, no! I don't need a stool or chair. You can bring out that stuff when the men from the police camp come. I am just a coolie,' said Angusami, and sat on one of the two raised platforms at the entrance.

'The way you put it, one would think that a lot of policemen visit this house. You do not know my father's nature. If any male came up here without a specific reason, well, it would be a different story altogether. When he decided that the room could be rented to you, father had determined there and then that you are a respectable man.'

'That's why the stool and chair are being pulled out for me!' said Angusami, coming closer to sit on the stool. As he did so, his body touched Tangammai.

'Oh no! I have touched you!' he laughed.

'Nothing wrong with it – it wasn't intended. You are not an untouchable, are you?'

'If you act so mature about such accidents, I don't need to worry... Who is this, in military uniform?' he asked, pointing to a large framed picture on the wall.

'He is the father of the child... he sent this picture. When this one was in my womb, he died in a plane crash... All that I got to see were his shirt and shoes and other clothing.' Angusami could see a film of tears in her eyes as she stood staring into the evening light.

'I wouldn't have asked you at all if I had known that it will cause you such grief...'

'It is of no value, this grief of mine. All I worry about now is this child and her upbringing. She should be entrusted to a good man... that's my goal in life.'

'But your father is here to take care of the problem. So you shouldn't worry much.'

'Father is no longer a young man. You seem to think that perhaps the house and the grove belong to father.'

'They don't?'

'All this is government land which we have been enjoying for some years. During the season, the government takes away the produce, and we get a few mangoes and coconuts that last but a few days. Father has no other income.'

'Now I get the full picture. It's difficult, no doubt. I should be going now, I've been here for a long time. I shall come again when your father is here.'

'No, no. It was wrong of me to talk such a lot and forget to offer a Wednesday visitor even a glass of water. Give me five minutes...' said Tangammai, disappearing into the kitchen.

❖

Her friendly conversation, and her straightforward questions and answers created ripples in the calm of Angusami's mind. Since he had moved here, he had started to feel something blooming within him; he sensed a new energy. The green of the grove, the cool dawns, the hustle and bustle of the market – everything had acquired a new sheen that portended a sweet joyfulness.

Sitting on the chair, Angusami contemplated his tiny dwelling. Born in a dry, unyielding land, he had starved, struggled and survived somehow. He had pushed on and gradually, there grew within him the thought that he was alone in the world. Suddenly, in this tiny abode, his mind felt cool and calm. The woman had once lived with a man and lost him, and she was left with a maimed child to take care of. She had nobody of her own, except her ageing father...

As Angusami contemplated his own strength and the stretch of life that lay ahead of him, a new hope sprang up in him.

'Goodness, it is evening. I must light the lamp...The girl is still sleeping. She is perhaps feeling lonely. Here's some tea for you, with goat's milk. Hope you like it.' Tangammai held out a glass of hot tea to him, smiling.

'I like any milk. But it should not be adulterated, that's all.' He threw her a well-aimed, meaningful look and began to sip the tea.

'We do not trade in milk. So there is no need to adulterate. The milk is good. How is the tea?'

'Since the person who made the tea is good, so is the tea.'

'How did you decide that the person is good?'

'Well... I know of a certain trick to determine if a person is good...'

'Then you have not found a good one all these days?'

'Only in a crowd. Seeing one, and that too properly – that is only now.'

'Aiyo, then one had better be careful. Having seen a real one, he shouldn't venture to kidnap that one in the middle of the night.'

'This Angusami is not the sort that will come prowling in the dead of right... he'll come straight, so straight – that is his habit.'

'So, now there is going to be some straightforward action?'

'Yes... when the time comes, I shall eschew the reason and come.'

'Quite a smart man.' Tangammai laughed heartily. So did Angusami, forgetting himself.

Inside, the little girl woke up with a whimper.

'The little wretch is awake. It will be a night vigil for me, like Sivaratri. Let me light the lamp. Do not leave now.'

The girl came out of the room and stepped down, runny-nosed and weeping in a crumpled cotton skirt and blouse. At a moment when he had been feeling so joyous, this black apparition had turned up like a black ant creeping into paradise. An immeasurable hatred against her welled up in him. In the light of the hurricane lamp that Tangammai brought along, that ugliness was magnified several-fold. And its mother was a charming, cultured, good-natured woman... Why did he not...in those heady first moments...weigh the pros and cons in this fashion, as he was doing now. And that hatred stuck, like a deep scar.

Fifteen

Those pleasant moments that had touched life so fleetingly…to recall them, lying down, forgetting the real world…When he was compelled to stay in bed, these sweet memories coiled and unravelled again and again.

Even while awake, he was reliving the exuberance of those days. As the reality of his present surroundings slowly intruded into his awareness, he felt a sense of sorrow seep in from everywhere. He felt helpless.

'Angusami Mooppan! Asleep, at the sunset hour? Open your eyes and see who all are here!'

Angusami opened his eyes slowly and focused them on the crowd of men around him.

'The whole lot of you! Please, please sit down. Sit down…' He turned over on his side and sat up with the support of his right arm.

'Mooppan should get up carefully, there is no hurry…' said the visitors. Covering the upper part of her body with a soot-darkened towel, Panki peeped from the kitchen.

'Girl, didn't you tell Mooppar that we were planning to come here?'

'Father was in deep sleep when I came home. I didn't want to disturb him. You have all come, anyway... Damodara Anna will be here after he has changed. I thought that he would come and tell him...'

'You go inside, girl, and bring something to drink... Tea, water, whatever they want... As the days go by, my weakness is only increasing. I have been in bed for a month now. The swelling seems to subside, but is back every morning and throbs with pain. These days, the doctor comes on alternate days. He massages the area with oil and he is satisfied with it. Well something is bound to happen... Let all that be, for the moment. Let's know the purpose of this visit. I see that our boat contractor and the "boat chief" Vallam Mooppan are here...'

'Mooppare, we are going to tell you right away. So it is only the swelling that troubles you now – are you okay otherwise? We have to know that first.' Vallam Mooppan unwound the thin towel covering his head and wiped his face.

'Nothing wrong with my health. But I am mentally depressed. Now that's a big setback...'

'That's the matter! To solve that problem, we have come here with good intentions. We are celebrating the Madan festival on the riverfront for ten days, starting on the fifteenth of this month. Every year, you used to dance and get into a trance at the festival. This year it cannot be so. If that is Madan's will, so be it. At least during the next festival, if He wills you to do the ritual dance, you will do that. Why "if?" He will. Now, each one of us is contributing two rupees, at the pier. We have to collect a little more, from the interior too.

There is a lot of expenditure. As special attractions, we are getting a dummy-horse dancer from Alwarkurichi in Pandiya Nadu, and pancha vadhyam percussionists from the Kerala Kala Manram.

'The parties will perform free for us, but we have to pay for their travel. All other things have been taken care of by donors. We are enrolling you in the festival committee. That's why we are here – to tell you that and to enquire about your health. This is a public initiative for a holy purpose. One should bear with everything and be hopeful that everything will turn out for the better. If you say that you are tired, you stay tired. You can walk. You can slowly walk to the pier and back. Your mind will feel better, you will feel hopeful... Another important piece of news... We are including your Damodaran also in the committee...'

Angusami sat listening. Then they left, after telling him what his responsibilities were. Damodaran had joined them and left. Panki served him dinner and went to sleep in the kitchen. It was very dark. A dog barked far away. Out in the grove, the crickets raged on with their endless, monotonous percussion.

Sleep eluded Angusami. He had overslept during the day, which he ought not to have done. Since he had fallen ill, there was no planned activity for the day. So it was sleep during the day and wakefulness at night... Such was his luck.

The small sum that he had put away was being spent on the doctor's fees and the medicinal oil. Thanks to Panki, they were managing to meet the daily expenses. Heaven knew what sin he had committed that it was her earnings which should provide him with his daily gruel. From the moment he had happened to see her till this moment, all that he had felt for her was pure hatred. But how did he accept it when the creature gave him his food, kept water ready for his use, handed him the tooth scrub, smoothed and prepared his bed, and gave him his oil and medicine? Not once did his heart soften and never had he deigned to see her with compassionate eyes... For him, this was a relationship that was not in the least sought after, it was a connection to be rooted out, a burden not to be borne... One look at Tangammai and he had instinctively given her a place in his heart. But the revulsion he had felt when he had seen this uncouth creature the first time was like a black blanket of hatred that overwhelms one's sensibilities when one bends down to strangle an unwanted animal.

Before he knew it, Angusami was overcome by sleep in the midst of these thoughts.

Sixteen

The river flowed clean and clear. Beneath the wide blue of the sky, it gleamed like blue glass.

It was the ninth day of the Madan festival. On the next day, the tenth, things were bound to become utterly chaotic. All the boats were arrayed neatly from the bank up to the point where the rivers took an eastward course. On the cement platform of the old casuarina tree, a statue, as tall as a man, had been erected. It was painted and decorated impressively by the Nayudu from Sivakasi. He held a trident, a whip and a scythe, and had fearsome canines, matted hair, four arms, a blood-red tongue, and eyes that spewed rage. Nearby stood his consort, a yakshi. She was painted to look like Mahishasuramardhini, and exuded unchallengeable bravery and righteous rage. All around the temple, flat-roofed pandals had been put up. On one side of the deity lay the golden flowers of the kamugu tree, bunches of bananas and green coconuts, garlands of the red thetti flowers and heaps of vermillion powder, on brass plates. There was a cage containing several cocks, to be sacrificed in eight directions the next day.

Though the sun was scorching hot, men and women came from near and far, alone and in groups, to pray to Madan Tampuran. They made good their pledges to the god in front of the collection boxes and smeared some vermillion powder on their foreheads and those of the children, as prasada. Many of them put silver or gold miniatures of an eye, an arm or a leg into a bronze boat-shaped container that stood next to Madan Sami. In Panki's case, it was a silver arm, praying as she was for Angusami's speedy recovery. Festival shops had sprung up all along the bank, which had earlier been covered with sand hillocks. There were some eateries, and ribbons, bangles, tassels, vermillion paste, kohl, colourful decorations made of palm leaves, aluminium, bronze and brass vessels, ready-made clothes and peanuts were being sold here, making the place a virtual marketplace. All the shops had jute curtains to keep the sun out.

At night, all the petromax lights came to life, spilling their reflections on the water. Come evening and the place would be seized by a new energy. Groups of men would play dice games, their lusty shouts accompanying each throw of the dice that rattled inside a tin can. Others played card games. Four men, clad in white waist cloths and white fanned turbans, sang praises of Madan, keeping rhythm with large cymbals. From the surrounding groves, like East Arannur, Ilangam, Valiyalilai and Pavangodu, women and children gathered together at the river for the festival. The local folk bought themselves new shirts and waist cloths even if they had to borrow money. They sometimes gave up on the idea of buying new apparel for Onam, but the Madan festival was too special for them. Madan Tampuran of the riverfront was their biggest god, the god who answered their call. Pox, fever, cholera, the worst of diseases or come what may, their Madan dispelled it with one puff of his breath.

The competing percussion groups of northern Kerala created an extraordinary din. The noise pierced through one's eardrums and drove many into a state of delirium. Young men would dance, unstoppable and with their hair flying, as the spirit of Madan possessed them. The riverfront would thus pulsate with a chaotic energy.

Seventeen

Seated on a bench in the shed, Angusami took a look at the swirling activity on the riverfront and fixed his eyes on the river, which flowed quietly. It was like a mother shedding silent tears of joy for her happy children, serene and silent even as the men it had reared surrendered themselves to joyous revelry. Like a coconut kernel is filled with water, the river fills itself with sand and gives it freely and quietly, like a nursing mother. Angusami had shaved and bathed, and had worn a half-sleeved shirt and the Chengottai veshti with a double border. Though he had wanted to walk to the venue, Damodaran and the festival committee did not agree to his request. So he travelled in a cart, pulled by two oxen, to reach his work shed. The cart belonged to a sand contractor.

As soon as the cart came to a halt, ten men rushed to welcome him. Some of them had not known of his illness and some had not been able to visit him at home. Fond words of enquiry and consolation poured out of their mouths.

'Nothing much by way of improvement,' replied Angusami.

'It will take some more days to become normal...and I have not come to the riverfront for ages...It's like returning from a visit to a foreign land. Make room for me, let the water touch my eyes...' Angusami walked down towards the river, hitching up his veshti. Damodaran and a second man cautioned him to take slow steps. They wanted to hold his hands, but Angusami forbade them to do so.

'Nobody need stop me when I am stepping into my mother's lap,' he said. Stepping into the water, he cupped his hands, filled them with water, swallowed a mouthful and wiped his face with the remaining water, closing his eyes.

'Now take me up,' he said, extending the rigid left arm and the good right.

Sitting in his work shed, Angusami could see a good part of the area around him. At a distance, the river flowed in two branches, which joined at Vallamedu plain, all dignity and no fanfare, resembling a calm sea. All the vessels stood in neat rows, like pearls packed in an ear of corn. A couple of passenger boats ferried people from the opposite bank to join the festivities.

They had stored bunches of bananas and green coconuts inside the shed. At the steps, many new men could be seen going to and fro. Damodaran and the other committee members approached Angusami for advice every now and then. Kadambu Ramanuja Pillai, who played the nadaswaram for the festival year after year, met Angusami and paid his respects. He put his pipes, the tavil drum and a few other things in a corner of the shed.

Angusami's heart fluttered when he remembered that he would not be performing the ritual dance and would be confined to his house.

His back began to ache since he had sat for so long. He had become too used to resting in bed for long stretches... He called out to a man who happened to be passing by. 'Who is that? The younger Narayanan? I have to lean on something... Can you bring those cotton spreads?...'

'Most certainly, I shall do so right away. Our Mooppan should regain his strength. There is still time for our guests to arrive...' He quickly piled up the cotton spreads, meant to be used by the invitees, and the palm leaf bundles and gently propelled him to the makeshift couch.

Angusami felt relaxed and shut his eyes. He managed to sleep a little. Thoughts crossed his mind as he hovered between sleep and wakefulness, in an in-between stage. The thoughts occurred with clarity, like goldfish swimming in a glass tank... The riverfront festival was an important event. His friends had shown him such respect, taken no notice of his infirmity and given him a respectable position on the committee. It was all due to this river-mother. The river originated in an unknown dark crevice in the mountain, came down through crags and crannies, and finally created spacious banks. It was famous for the settlements flourishing on its banks and for the flawless way it flowed. Did it matter that the river originated in an unknown spot? It is where it flows and the places that it enriches that bring it fame. Was he not like that, too? He was born in a remote corner of Tamil territory, its memory all but forgotten and even its dregs having evaporated. He grew up here, worked, made money, and enjoyed a degree of well-earned fame and respect. Angusami felt a thrill go over his body as he pictured, with his mind's eye, the river in its entirety... He then drifted off into sleep.

He was woken up by some movements near him and opened his eyes. Someone whispered and someone laughed, very softly. Behind a boat that had not been fully built and stood upright, a man and woman were changing. They must be the karagam artistes, who danced with pots balanced on their heads, thought Angusami upon seeing a tinsel-bordered jacket with a brightly coloured bodice.

'You girl, you are so clumsy with the jacket. Bring it here, I'll help you into it. This is a Kerala town. If you don't look fetching, nobody will bother to throw even a glance...'

'What's so special about the Malayalis? Do they have horns on their heads? Men are the same, wherever they may be... I, for one, can say that...'

'Indeed, how many men have you seen, and in how many towns, my little princess...' He slipped into glittery pantaloons and pinched her cheeks playfully.

'Look here, right from the minute we caught the train, you have been "busy" with your hand. Don't you think that I am not aware of it. More of this "hand" and I shall call uncle...'

He knew only too well that this anger was fake.

'You will call "uncle"... Call him, right now...' he said. Moving his hand quickly to reach her back, he unhooked her bodice deftly.

'Aiyo, you have no sense of shame. It is evening, the lights are yet to be lit... the performance has to take place... What's wrong with you? Have you made a trip to the liquor shop or what?' she said, albeit in an enticing tone, covering her body with her sari and holding the bodice from coming loose.

Angusami found it funny and wanted to laugh. A curious feeling swept over him as he heard the sound of the Pandiya Nadu Tamil. It meant something, certainly. Here, it was only his name that was a Tamil word.

'Look there, an elderly man is asleep, leaning there . . . what sort of a man are you? Put your art on display after scanning the audience, wise men say . . . and it is not for nothing.'

Realizing that he had been indiscreet, the man quickly changed his manner of talking. 'Be quick now. You brought these anklet bells that are stitched on to leather belts? They'll never shake, however high you jump . . .' Suddenly, he displayed great alacrity in his movements.

'Great people! Showing so much involvement in their calling once they know there is someone here,' said Angusami, clearing his throat and sitting up straight. The man and the woman were scared out of their wits.

'Who are you? Where are you from?' Angusami spoke in a loud voice, conveying annoyance.

The young man asked him who he was, with a touch of hesitation.

'So you'll answer only if you know who I am? I am a member of the festival committee. And you? Are you a dummy-horse dancer?'

'No, we do the karagam dance, she and I, balancing pots on our heads. Our elder must not think badly of us,' he said. He hastened to rub off the excess paint on his hand. The girl, with tell-tale eyes that were red and bleary, was drawing black semi-circles on her eyebrows.

'I did not see anything. Why should I misunderstand you?' He smiled and leaned back.

The pain seemed to have increased. Outside, on the riverfront, the festival was assuming new colours.

Panki, clad in a new waist cloth, a green jacket and an upper cloth with a border decorated with a design of leaves, entered the room, chatting with two girls. He turned to face the other side and shut his eyes tight, feigning sleep. He was not in the least desirous of seeing that face, that black iron pot decorated with dots of white lime, as he described her to himself.

Eighteen

When Tangammai was alive, he had visited the Madan festival with her a couple of times. But he had been too burdened with responsibilities and had not had the time to visit shops or share light-hearted moments, like so many other young couples did.

He found that he derived greater satisfaction recalling the past, which was inhabited by her, than things related to his present life. Those memories were like unstoppable waves, returning again and again, as he slowly retreated from the outer world and hovered just beyond the border of consciousness, almost sleeping, or when sleep eluded him despite all his efforts…

❖

Tangammai was sitting in front of him. She had taken a bath and applied a dot of holy ash on her forehead. Her long hair, which came down to her waist, had been gathered in a small knot at the ends. She wore a clean white waist cloth and a light red blouse. No jewellery adorned her. Her neck was bare and there was nothing on her wrists, not even glass bangles. Nor did she wear a nose pin. The contours of her blouse ignited his mind. Tangammai shone like a yakshini, the semi-divine female spirit.

Tangammai was sitting in front of him…

'What is this, why do you stare as though I am a stranger?'

Angusami was scratching the black enamel rim of the plate with his nail.

'Eat the rice. I have made a thick kozhambu with onions and freshly roasted and ground condiments. Mix it properly and eat well. A working man – if he doesn't eat well and keeps staring at somebody…well, that's good work that he is doing…All that it will do is to push dusk to dawn.'

'So be it, Tangammai. Let it become dawn. Your father has entrusted me with your care today…The reason is that he trusts me. I cannot betray him. So…just stay there, don't move…Let me just look at you for some more time…'

'Still, for how long can one keep staring at someone? Today is the last Thursday of the month. When the bhajans start at the temple, my nerves will go slack…This has happened every month since Panki's father died. If my father had not trusted you, he wouldn't have told a man to take care of me…He can hardly refuse to accompany the IG, can he?'

'I have been wanting to ask god Hanuman for a few boons. There appears to be a good opportunity today…But Hanuman won't appear till I finish dinner…What's this here, fried fish?'

'Good god, today is not a day for fish, curried or fried. Even if the stuff is flying in the air, we do not get fish or meat on Thursdays... This is an eggplant, toasted in coconut oil. You are a man from Pandiya Nadu. At long last, I got an opportunity to feed you and today, of all days, could make at least a kozhambu for you. But going by the way you are moving your hand on the plate, it seems you don't find it tasty... I suppose you'll eat it only if I mush it up for you and divide it into fitting mouthfuls.'

'Don't do either. All this is a sin, towards Hanuman and a trusting father.'

'Heaven knows how long I'll remain like this, considering issues of sin and virtue. All said and done, Pandiya Nadu fellows are not to be trusted. What's more, I am the mother of a child who has neither looks, nor brains... That's my crime.' Tangammai was on the verge of crying.

'Look, Tangammai, I am a Tamil; yes, from Pandiya Nadu. But I am not one who does not keep his word. In this lived-in room, in front of this food, I tell you that we will be man and wife, with the full knowledge of the world. How does it matter if you are the mother of a child? The person I am going to marry is you, a woman full of affection. I promise...'

From the other side of the wall, the policemen began singing bhajans, softly at first. The conch was sounded and then came the clanging of bells, which set off a tingling sensation in the inner ear. In a high-pitched refrain, the rough voices intoned the various names of god, totally out of tune with the notes of the harmonium and the cymbal beats. The notes took off in a wayward manner, like a calf that has run off with the tether. 'Eternal celebate, Sri Rama's servant, Every day we pray, That you may guard us,' went the words.

In the dim light of dusk the tall coconut palms trembled like swords of silver. The breeze swept in the scent of parijata flowers from the tree that grew near the well. The leaves of the mango tree appeared to be dancing. The young fruit looked like dark pendulums receding into the dark. The singing reached a crescendo… The metallic strumming of a stringed instrument seemed to touch the inner ear, impacting on the nerves. The scent of frankincense floated in.

Nineteen

Tangammai was smiling and sitting in front of Angusami. On the dull-looking wall was the photograph of the man in uniform. The hurricane lamp emitted a bright light. In a corner, Panki lay asleep, curled up under a crumpled sheet. Her cleft lip joined her nose and her breathing was loud and unpleasant. Her rough, dry hair and graceless posture made her appearance all the more unpalatable. Had Tangammai, too, distanced herself from the girl…? He had to somehow ignore this thought, set it aside and take the matter in his stride…

After Tangammai and he had drawn close and shared their thoughts with each other, what was it that prevented him from seeking her physical touch, to make her his, legitimately? Was it this 'child'? Angusami sometimes felt that Tangammai's father wanted such a relationship to grow between them, for he was out on many nights, either working in the camp, going on sudden trips with officials, or attending to special cooking duties or something else. Tangammai behaved with propriety and not like a creature allowed to 'graze' freely. And Angusami always remembered not to cross the line of propriety as he was well past the age of restless youthfulness. Even on those occasions when their conversations entered forbidden ground, Tangammai did not step out of her ramparts to cling to him. She always spoke like an innocent and shy girl, unaware of 'worldly' knowledge. She displayed a restrained possessiveness towards him. Also, she did not fail to express her heartfelt desires when the opportunity arose. This was one such day.

She was quite surprised that the Hanuman bhajan did not affect her in any way that evening. She had tried earlier not to succumb to that impulse by resolving to be strong and poised, and by even rejecting all thoughts of faith in the god... But the moment the chorus would begin and subsequently reach a thunderous crescendo, she would break into a cold sweat, and recoil and withdraw into herself. Darkness would shroud her eyes and her throat would turn dry. Her mind would be sucked into a vortex and she would swoon. Then she would see Hanuman in his viswarupa form, filling her eyes and beyond. The chorus of voices would align with and coil around one another, tightly gripping each other, crazed. In a hazy state of awareness and amorphous ecstasy, on one side she would see the colourful image of the transcendental Hanuman and on the other, the line-up of well-built policemen... till her mindscape collapsed and she passed out, with a loud sound issuing from her throat.

...But today? Is this change the result of Angusami's nearness?

'Tangamme!'

'What?'

'Are you all right?'

'I'm fine. My mind is at peace. I am happy too. But I can't describe this happiness...'

'Why?'

'I am not able to...Maybe because...you're sitting so close.'

'Then come a little closer.'

'Oh no, I won't. Today is the last Thursday.'

'Look, Lord Hanuman himself, who was scheduled to arrive today, has stayed away for our sake...You come here, I tell you.'

'No, I'm afraid.'

'Afraid?'

'No...I feel shy,' she said, casting a glance at the picture on the wall and her daughter sleeping on the mat. Tears filled her eyes, which glistened in the dull light.

'Tangammai, if you and I get together, the person in that picture will definitely support it...Come here...'

Tangammai got up and stood in front of Angusami. He held her close to his chest.

On the other side of the wall, the activities in the Hanuman temple had come to an end. The viswarupa figure on the wall was not visible in the dark. A cool breeze swept through the greenery. Silence reigned all around.

A scream escaped the sleeping girl's throat and she sat bolt upright. Tangammai, till now lost to the world in Angusami's loving embrace, freed herself instantly and ran towards her.

'Daughter, why did you cry? Did you have a dream? Were you frightened?' She soothed her, stroking her body and laid her down.

Angusami was more than put off. A loving, affectionate

woman like Tangammai carried this inalienable burden, the burden of such a child. Hatred enveloped his whole being. It welled up, unstoppable, overwhelming him.

Twenty

The river flowed quietly, as always. Boats with familiar loads of sand, coconuts and husk crossed the water. Work had begun anew at a brisk pace on the riverfront after the Madan festival had ended. A passenger bus had hit the steel railing on the eastern side of the overbridge and knocked off a portion of it. After the last rains, nearly as much as a furlong of the high bank on the western side of the river had collapsed and fallen into the water. A stone wall had been erected to shore up the area. Nothing remained of the sand workers' hutments that had earlier dotted the place. A structure, which was intended to be a tile factory, was coming up there. The place wore a new look, with women carrying loads of bricks on their heads, bricklayers mixing concrete, and ironsmiths cutting and welding rods.

The work of trowelling sand from the river continued apace. Men and women bore baskets of wet sand shovelled from the riverbed, the dripping water drenching their heads, bodies and clothing. The sand was piled in huge heaps beneath the tree near the Madan temple. The price of coir rope, as also of coconut sheath, had gone up. Even the price of bricks had shot up. Those were 'good' days for contractors who sold half-baked bricks as it was possible to make a quick buck. But the price of sand did not go up beyond seven rupees a cartload. The workers made less money than their brethren elsewhere.

Angusami could not work much any more, though he had decided to return to the shed. He neither had the strength to order workers, what with his depleted lung power, nor to stick to his quoted price before buyers. This meant incessant arguments with prospective buyers. He used to be adept at arguing with them, but not any more. Something had gone in the intervening period of his illness. Even the urchin who assisted the cart driver had the cheek to say that Mooppan was not the way he used to be...

All he had to do was to note the names of the men and women who came to work, including Damodaran, and collect the money obtained from the sale of the sand. The contractor hardly required one person to do this job. However, he employed Angusami for the sake of old times. He often said that Angusami needed to retire from work.

True, Angusami also felt a deep desire to rest. His left arm still ached when he raised it. It was still not good enough to lift even the lightest of weights, not even a piece of coal.

His physical strength was like that of a boat with a hole in the bottom. Inevitably, the expanse of the world he inhabited shrank. Times were changing. Optimism and gratitude were no longer cherished values. Everyone was an escapist, looking for non-existent footprints on flowing water. When times are bad, even a tuber turns fibrous. His clean life, the respect he had been accorded, his pride at having held his head high at home and in the world outside...wherever had these values gone? Were the rest picking on him, the way an eagle is stoned by heartless men when it loses its flight? The contractor, the notables on the riverfront, the Madan temple trustees, boatmen, coolies, women...the whole lot seemed to look down on him. The fact that one of his arms was feeble seemed to have eaten into the strength of his entire body and his standing in society. They said one could see a thousand crows if one threw food on the roof. So what if he could not be there on the riverfront? There would be many like him to replace him. Nobody was ever unique and irreplaceable, realized Angusami. All he had left now was the past, a past spent in the lap of the river, after his days in the streets of the marketplace.

Twenty-one

'Son, you must stop carrying loads at the marketplace. It doesn't suit one beyond a point in time. This work is not suitable for good people. Now you are nearly thirty years old, I think. Now Tangammai also belongs to you. When you are a householder, you must have a respectable calling. Take my work, for example. I have always cooked for a living, as far as I can remember. I started out working in the Residency Bungalow as a helper, under a white sahib. Those were the days of British rule, with the viceroy and resident in power. Such great days, days of plenty! For two chakras one got a large measure of rice. One British rupee would last you a good fifteen days. Since I was working in the kitchen, there was no dearth of food. When I married Tangammai's mother, I had got a promotion and was working as the chief cook in the musafiri bungalow – the transit house – I could toss up anything, cutlets, chops, mutton fry, roast, bull's eye... with no effort at all. Once, an English officer staying in the bungalow had the mutton roast and wanted to see me even as he was being served at the table. I presented myself, looking like a statue in full uniform, complete with my headgear with its frilled "fan" on top, a shirt with cuffed sleeves and golden buttons, and pants. I stood at attention and saluted him. "What is your name?" he asked me. "My name is Kuttan Butler," I answered promptly, with full confidence and without any hesitation. The sahib was utterly pleased with my English, and madam just laughed and laughed. When the sahib left the bungalow, he gave me a sovereign – a little smaller in size than our whole silver rupee – and also wrote four lines praising me. He shook hands with me before he left. From then on, it was good times for me. I was attached to the corps, got a certificate and a presentation…

'Why I say this is that right now, I cook for the police camp. No one has any special regard for me, as they used to earlier. After Independence, the old royal touch and the Englishman's method and style blew away with the wind. Now cooking is a simple job. It's chapattis in the morning. There are sacks of atta. For lunch, it is chapatti with sambar and vegetable koottu. Twice a week, there is meat or fish. All this is child's play. But if you accompany senior officers to camps, it is back to British times. Let me tell you this, my son – only power has changed hands; otherwise, all the British ways are being followed…

'Angusami, I am an old man now…My eyesight is weak. My hearing too is poor. The other day, I emptied out an iron wok filled with sifted flour, mistaking it for water that had been used to wash rice. The store master ticked me off…It is no longer like before. Changes take place as time moves on. Even if you cook rice at midnight, it becomes "yesterday's rice" by the following morning. That's why son, I tell you…

"I found him, so let me keep him, confine him" is not what I intend for you. I've thought of something that you can do. You know Vallamedu, where the two rivers meet. There is good business there in sand. This year, the entire contract has been awarded to a Kottayam man, a mappila. He supplies firewood and spices to the camp. He also owns a few boats and nets. One is required to help the contractor. The man has a good opinion of me. As soon as he mentioned this, I thought of you. When he said that he was looking for someone who is firm, speaks tactfully, and is straightforward and trustworthy, I could honestly not think of anyone else. I said so to the gentleman. And that you are my son-in-law, that you are a respectable person hailing from Pandiya Nadu. He became partial towards you when he learnt that you are a Tamil. After I spoke in your favour, he had no objection whatsoever…

'Tomorrow happens to be the first day of the first month of the year, the Simha month of the Malayalam calendar. You should come along with me without a second thought. I'll fix everything. Tangammai suggested this long ago. She had once lived with a man of good social status and reputation. I too kept the company of English masters and police officers, and have lived well. So it is not the most ideal thing that you, who are like a son to me, should struggle as a coolie in the streets of the market. It's true that a person who calls himself a man can live with self-respect even if he collects waste to earn his bread, but this work is better. When the stars are favourable, there should be nothing to prevent one from buying a couple of boats and getting a contract. Tangammai, the poor girl, gave birth to a girl who does not have a normal appearance. That was decreed by fate. She too will need money at some point in her life. During my lifetime, we have eaten and dressed well. But there is not a paisa of savings. We occupy this government accommodation as long as I work…

'I think it is because of the good deeds I must have done in my past life that you have become a part of our household, though you are a Pandiya Nadu man. All I have is you and all you have is us. Were I to die today or ten days later, I would go with the assurance that our son will not forsake Tangammai and her daughter. I have seen many young men. Since I live so close to the police camp, I've seen many a mustachioed "he-man" take an interest in us. Whether they were open or sneaky, they did not impress me. You came to live in the room. I was observing you too…When she lay in a trance, overcome by the spirit of Hanuman, how you had come running! And you did not know whether you should touch her or not…and I've observed many other times…It didn't take me long to realize that you would not be disrespectful to women. It was then that I paid heed to Tangammai…After that military man died, she spent four-odd years alone with this unfortunate creature and observed severe austerities. There were proposals from a couple of persons, but she was not interested. She chose to be engrossed in the worship of Hanuman and was like an ascetic. She changed her mind only after she met you. Not because of your good looks…it's because of your dignity and measured speech…You should come to the riverfront tomorrow, to the pier…'

…A long time had passed since then! Tangammai's father, who had pulled him out of the morass of the marketplace to sacred river sands, was no more…

Angusami began to feel more and more that he was being surrounded by a void. Life on the riverfront had lost its charm as the place was increasingly being populated by insubstantial men who had little depth of character.

'Angusami Anna!' That was Damodaran calling him with his usual concern and affection. His voice seemed to come from a distance – a voice that conveyed a feeling of attachment as well as a sense of respect in an otherwise bleak environment of disregard.

Twenty-two

An ox-cart was making its way down the incline from the bridge, very slowly...The oxen were moving step by step. But they lost their sure-footedness since the pair of hands tugging at the rope were inexperienced. They began to run uncontrolled, pushed by the load behind them. The boy who was driving the cart screamed in fear, and everyone on the bank looked in that direction. A moment more and the cart, the boy and the animals would have fallen into the river...

Angusami lunged forward, jumped into the cart, tugged hard at the rope and managed to halt the animals. One of the wheels of the cart got caught in the slush and there was no further damage.

The men pushed the wheel up the bank, freed the animals from the yoke and tied them to a tree. Angusami asked the boy to sit on the bench in the shed and consoled him. 'Kid, who are you?' he asked him. 'Whose is the cart and the oxen? You are perhaps fifteen years old? Who is the man who entrusted you with this task? He must be really intelligent to have done this, I must say!'

'The cart belongs to Aranur Appu contractor. I live in that house. The animals do understand the language of my hands. His cart does a hundred rounds in the markets of Palayam and Mettukkadai...'

'You are good enough there, I am sure, but not for the riverfront. When you come down, you have to pull back the right and leave a loose leash for the left. Even a brief slip will plunge you and the cart into the water. Had I not stopped you, there would have been a total commotion here...'

That day he felt a sense of fulfilment...He had a woman he loved for a wife. The river had given him a new life, and he loved the new environment. Whatever he saw and did had a new glow. Wonderful days they were. The boy he had rescued also became a part of his life.

Damodaran was a tall, straight-backed young man now. His heart felt full whenever he looked at him. He was strong and spare, with a trim moustache and a head of curly hair, and was always neatly clad in a waist cloth and a vest. A man reared in the lap of the river.

After that occasion, Angusami saw him many times in the market and at the rail junction. 'You, cart-man! You're doing fine, I hope,' he would call out in a teasing tone. Their bond became close enough to lead Damodaran to Angusami's shed one day, while the latter was settling accounts. Damodaran stood before him with a bundle of clothes in his hand, his eyes wet.

'Hey, cart-man! What's the matter, you've been weeping... And this bundle...are you out on a pilgrimage?' He was inclined to tease him even at that moment.

As though waiting for this cue, the lad began to shed copious tears.

'Young man! Whatever happened to you? Tell me, c'mon, tell me now. Did the contractor hit you or something? Or did you do something wrong? Tell me now, honestly. Did you steal something? Whatever it is, tell me. I'll hear you out...'

The contractor was a good man, but his wife was a rough woman. She was constantly finding fault with him and often carped that what he did failed to measure up to what she fed him. On this day, she had gone a little further and beat him. And the contractor – and this had really hit him – had not bothered to take any interest in the matter or even uttered a word to soften the blow. He could no longer tolerate that place, which was so blatantly devoid of affection, which set no store by loyalty. Though there was no one in his village whom he could call his own, he had decided to go back.

'Let all that be now. Why do you want to go back? And do what there? Let me ask you that first...'

'There's nothing there, but there's nothing here either.'

'Is this your decision or has the contractor ordered you to leave town?'

'No, no, he said nothing of the kind.'

'In that case, you can stay here, if you get work!'

'Yes, of course I can. I can do any work.'

'We'll think about it. For the moment, wait. You can go home after giving it proper thought.'

When he brought him home, Tangammai's father voiced his doubts. 'Times are different and you are the type who's moved quickly. Even the clear river water turns muddy when it rains...'

'I did not bring him as a house servant. I want to find him

some work at the pier. He is a fine young boy on the verge of adulthood... Everyone need not be blessed with a fine father and mother... It's one's fate, no more and no less. He needs care. He's also someone like me, I thought, and brought him here.'

'Not that I wanted to find fault with you... You are a hard-working man. I merely told you to think twice... One needn't say much to a thinking man.'

Twenty-three

The river nurtured Damodaran too. He was an active young man and he spoke in a measured tone. He was disciplined in his habits.

Damodaran bore loads of sand on his head. He worked under the boatman day and night in the sand boats and in the boats that crossed the river to and fro. He helped load sand in the carts and carried bricks in the kiln. Time made a man of him, too.

When Tangammai's father took ill and became bedridden, it was Damodaran who began to live in Angusami's room and served the old man. The latter, who had spent his whole life in front of kitchen fires, was stricken with gout and needed support to lift his body and move about. Damodaran did everything possible to help the old man. After he came home from the river, he would help Tangammai. He'd fetch water from the well, buy spices from the shop, get fish from the evening market. He played with Panki, whom even the neighbours avoided. He took her to school and picked her up. When she was rejected by the school as a below-normal child because of her disability, it was Damodaran who cared for her. On days, he did not go to the river to work; he would take the goat for grazing and Panki accompanied him. He would tell her stories, like 'The diver and the djinn' and 'One mother, ten children'. Panki devoured the latter story, which he narrated with embellishments. The last of the ten children was not pretty. But a prince came from across the seven seas, fell in love with her and married her.

Panki always identified herself with this girl. 'Anna,' she would tell Damodaran, 'tell me the story of that girl who wasn't good-looking.'

'Panki is really fond of the "ten children story". She thinks she will be visited by a prince who will marry her,' he would tell Tangammai, poking fun at Panki.

'Well, Damodaran,' Tangammai would say, 'You'll have to graze the goat as well as Panki.'

After Kuttan Mestiri died, Damodaran took care of Panki, who was like a blight in the married life of Angusami and Tangammai. As soon as Angusami and Damodaran returned from the river, the latter would take Panki to his room. He would light the lamp and tell her to recite the names of Lord Rama. He would encourage her to spell out words and read from her old books. They would cover up the goat pen with leaves.

'Come here and drink up your gruel, both of you, and let me wind up my work for the day,' Tangammai would call out. It was only then that Panki would step into the house. Despite the care that was taken to limit Panki's appearances before Angusami to a bare minimum, she was still the cause of bitterness and an occasional fight between Angusami and

Tangammai. One such incident occurred at the marketplace during a religious festival.

Angusami was not in favour of taking Panki along with them. 'We're going there to enjoy ourselves... Why take that creature along with us, as though we want to exhibit her before the whole wide world? That's why I don't like going out,' said an irritated Angusami.

'Now, to whom do you wish me to entrust her? This is a festival that happens only once a year. Damodaran is also coming with us. He can hold her by the hand...'

'Look Tangammai, he is a young boy. He too should get a chance to take a look around. As it is, he spends a lot of time with her every day. If he has to drag her along with him, he'll feel embarrassed. And anyway, he is an independent lad, capable of earning some money of his own. Is it his destiny to be offering us free labour? He may not say such things, but we ought to know... it's only human...'

'Well, you brought him along and you have great concern for him. As for her, I bore her and I have brought her up. She was not a foundling that I picked up from the river,' said Tangammai and began to weep.

'Did I ever say that you did not give birth to her? I married you though you were the mother of such a creature. She gets in the way of our spending a few carefree moments together on an outing and I say so as a matter of fact. Should you be crying because I am telling you the truth?'

'If she cannot go, I cannot either,' said Tangammai, and stepped back into her room.

'Anna, I overheard everything. Why argue over something so unimportant? It is for me to decide if being with Panki will ruin my fun. I am quite happy if she comes along with me.

She's like my own sister. Let's all go to the festival. You don't have to trouble yourself over her. If I buy her peanuts and a pinwheel, she'll stay by my side. As for me, I am not crazy about anything. When our king rides the chariot, he can be seen from anywhere in the throng. And that's all I wish to see. It's fine by me if you want me to stay at home with her... There she goes... she has started whimpering...!'

Tangammai was not inclined to leave the house after her father's death. He had been the sheet anchor of her life at times when it had seemed like an irredeemable abyss of darkness. Her life had been graced with light again when Angusami had fallen in love with her and married her. When her father died, she was filled with loneliness and sorrow, which were somewhat mitigated by Angusami's affection. She was worried that their life as a couple would be scarred by the bitterness that welled up between them due to her daughter. Angusami was a young man, in the prime of his life. He wished to enjoy life in every way and naturally, hated all impediments. During these awkward days, Damodaran became a source of solace for Tangammai.

Twenty-four

Wiping off all traces of bitterness, they put on new clothes and went to the festival. Tangammai and Angusami walked ahead, followed by Damodaran, who walked with Panki's hand in his. Like a 'grown-up', Damodaran had decided in favour of a waist cloth instead of his usual pair of knickers. Everyone whom they knew along the way made it a point to tease the two. 'Good, my boy! Let this little girl grow up some more and you'll make a fine couple!' Damodaran smiled in return, as he always did. As a habit, he never laughed aloud.

The marketplace was overflowing with people who had come from afar and places close by. There was an undulating sea of people at the eastern gate of the fort, from which descended an immense flight of stairs leading to the street that stretched ahead. All along the shop-lined street, there were colourful decorations with paper flags, traditional welcome arches adorned with green banana trees, tall bronze lamps lit with several wicks, huge pictures of the king and banners wishing him a long life.

Every year at the conclusion of the Navaratri festival, the ruling king, accompanied by men on elephants and horses and the foot soldiers, would climb into a large chariot in front of the Padmanabhaswami temple. He would go to the Puja hall three miles away and perform the ritual signalling the end of the religious celebrations. Though the country had gained independence and had become a republic, these royal processions continued to be held with as much fanfare as in earlier years. It was rumoured that this year's festival was to be the last such event. Angusami, who was not too fond of throngs and meaningless activity, had decided to witness the event for that reason alone. He also wanted Tangammai, who was constantly grieving for her father, to go for an outing. Far from making anyone happy, the outing ended on a sour note. Panki managed to free herself from Damodaran and got lost in the crowd.

Damodaran, red in the face, looked for her everywhere. 'I was right here. She wanted peanuts. She was missing when I looked up after taking out the change…'

'She will be back. Somebody is bound to bring her to us. Nobody is going to kidnap that beauty,' said Angusami, peering into the crowd. Such happy faces! And here he was… thanks to that ugly creature.

Tangammai's eyes were like pools of water and she struggled hard to keep herself from crying loudly. Damodaran looked here and there, with no results…

To signal the beginning of the event, a carriage drawn by a single horse sped past. As the crowd separated, the road, strewn with sand, could be seen stretching out far ahead. Just then a policeman came up to them, holding Panki by the hand, with Damodaran in tow.

'If you have to bring children to crowded places, you should be watchful. Hold her hand at least now.' Advising them thus, the policeman left. The festival held no interest for anyone after this unwelcome incident and it was a highly unpleasant walk back home.

Panki! She was the iron weight he had tied to his ankle, knowingly. The more he thought about her, the more weighed down he felt.

Twenty-five

'What are you thinking about so deeply? I have made rice for you. Come and eat, then you can think all you want.'

'Rice? What's so great about it? Don't we have it all the time? What if I didn't eat, for once?'

'I've noticed that lately, you've become more and more philosophical and withdrawn. You don't like me so much any more... It has not escaped my attention...'

'There you go! What's happened, all of a sudden? I didn't say that I won't eat. And you have concluded that I don't like food, that I am withdrawn... Next, you'll be calling me a mendicant or ascetic. Why don't you say that too and complete the story of my life? Look here, Tangammai! From the crack of dawn, we are playing with the river, sand and mud. Each hour is different from another. I might have left home smiling. And I may return home venting my spleen. Women who stay home don't know this. They think that their husbands come home to eat and for some other chores...'

'The more you talk, the more indiscreet you become...' said Tangammai, her lips curving in a coy smile.

'I am not being indiscreet. I am stating frankly what women think to themselves...All right, bring the rice and enamel dish. Let's eat together.'

'Yes, yes! Either the teacher stands on top of one's head or leaves the fray altogether, as the saying goes. Your behaviour bears out the validity of this saying. That girl will be lying awake. She needn't see this drama. You eat first... I'll eat later.'

'You use the girl as a good excuse for everything. She would have slept by now. Come here...'

'It is not exactly the second day of our marriage today. We've been married for five years.'

'But Tangammai, you'll always be a new woman for me. I don't even want you to become a mother...'

'Yes, indeed! As though our having or not having children is in our hands! I did not spend even ten days with that man and I had a girl no one wants. It's all god's will...'

Angusami did not fail to notice the tears welling up in her eyes. 'If we talk further, you will begin to cry. Here, come near me.'

'When you hear this, you wonder if this is the same man who was sitting here just now with a long face... You can put the rice on my palm... Do you have to make a ball out of it and put it into my mouth?'

'Tangammai, do you know how you look now?'

'Like a mother of ten children?'

'If one says that, one's throat will get parched for want of water. Tell me the truth. Did you actually give birth to this girl or did that military man drop her into your lap from some other place?'

Tangammai's cheerful face wilted immediately. Her pain was visible.

Angusami embraced her.

'Stop this nonsense... with all that food in your hand ... Didn't I tell you that it is not the second day of our marriage...?'

'Good... The crybaby smiled and drank up the milk!...'

'Child's play, indeed! If you have had your fill, get up and wash your hand. I have work to do...'

'Goodness, if you turn off the light like that, I won't be able to find the matchbox when I need it!'

'You don't need anything – matchbox or light. Let the day dawn. The light will come of its own.'

The sound of Tangammai's laughter added to the magic of the night for a long time.

❖

'Tangammai, today Damodaran pulled a young woman's hand...'

'No, Akka! Annan is teasing me!'

'Ei, did you or did you not touch Kamalakshi's hand?'

'Kamalakshi asked me to help her hold her basket up. By chance my fingers touched her ear. That's why Annan is saying all this. Anna, what will Akka think of me now? Annan is teasing me unthinkingly.'

'You and your Anna have no concern about what is the right time or place to play your pranks and games. And your Anna, he is apparently at the height of his youth. Go to your room and rest.'

'Don't drive him away so soon, Tangammai. If you are in a

hurry to shut the door and sleep, I'll come in. You don't have to shoo him off.'

'You can act quite ignorant sometimes. He is a young lad. Why should you act like his chum? He's just a nobody, a hanger-on.'

'Damodaran is our boy, whatever be our condition, and I can tell you that without a doubt. He is growing up, but he is a child at heart. He is not like your girl, who likes to hide from people before her eleventh year.'

'Come what may, your day is not complete if you don't carp at that girl.'

'Tangammai, you may think whatever you like. I dislike the very sight of that girl.'

'What's to be done now? Had I known that life would take such a turn, I'd have strangled her and killed her. It would have borne out the truth of the age-old saying that the child who dies while being born dies to let the mother live. Now she hears foul words in return for my happiness...'

'Enough, enough. If you start crying, everything else will go down the drain. Come, smile a little, just a little,' Angusami would say, encircling her waist. Damodaran would slink away as though nothing had happened.

Such lively moments...

Tangammai everywhere, at all times. With him in his sleep, in the working day, in his dreams and even in his bones... thrilling him, making him so happy... Golden days that were bedecked with flowers... He could dream on and on...

Twenty-six

'Mooppan, you have dozed off in your seat and are laughing away, to boot! I have been waiting for a few days now . . . You just sit and sleep.'

The man who spoke was a middle-aged coolie who took the sand off pebbles and pieces of rotting wood. He was smiling at Angusami.

'Who's that? . . . You! Bhargavan . . . So this day too has arrived, when I have become the target of your laughter. So be it. All that I am able to do now is sit . . . The contractor would love to send me back home. I can't get into the river for a few more days. How long can one sit planted on the bench, looking at numbers and notes? So one falls asleep – that's only natural. And there's no dearth of dreams, when it's afternoon sleep. So you will laugh at me, and so will someone who's younger still. So be it. Have you seen Damodaran?'

'Damodaran and your daughter are heaving loads at the eastern pier. There is less and less sand in the riverbed these days. Times are bad.'

'Nothing of the sort. It's our own doing. They put rocks near the pier and built a wall since the bank collapsed. And here, they constructed a bridge that dredged the bottom, where the two rivers would deposit sand. The river never fails... It is man who invents one solution after another. What can the river do about it? Earlier, it used to be ten to fifteen boatloads of sand each day. Now there aren't even three loads, even when you plunge deep...'

'Mooppar, you are right. But we want the bridge. And we want a strong embankment. Or else the water will flood the valleys in the rainy season. Then we'll have to eat straw, not paddy. We want this and that and the other. Earlier, we used to have fifty men working at one time. Now there are only ten or fifteen men, and all they do is to take a dip in the river... There is more slush than sand...And that too who knows for how long?'

'True, so what should one do? If we stop doing this work, as the contractor says, what is one to do?'

'That's not the right question to ask. In the Aranur region, the coconut crop is good and fetches a good price. There is plenty to do as well. Coconut that is grown within a six-mile radius is collected at this spot. At least ten boatloads cross to the other shore each day. There is nothing coming from Ceylon, apparently...The oil is in great demand and coir is being spun in every house. I am merely responding to Mooppar's words that one who has trusted the river is not let down by it. There is no sand in the river, but there are more on the banks...These here are three boatloads of sand. After being cleaned, they will make only two cartloads. That's what I have to tell you...'

'Bhargava, you are right. There is money in the coconut

and fibre business. The coir rope business is good all over the country. But how does that help us? We know only how to dive into the river; can we climb a coconut tree?'

When Panki and Damodaran returned home, the conversation proceeded along similar lines. They too began to talk about the changes taking place on the riverfront.

'Anna, you may not be aware of the latest since you have been laid up…Things have changed so much that what we now see is the reverse of what used to be. There is no work at the sand pier – nothing worth mentioning. The contractors are quite depressed. The younger men have even proposed that the boats should go to the sea for fishing. People lose hope in no time. When they face losses in business, they think of leaving their country. When they were profiting from mining, they had no second thoughts. Whatever that may be, we have to look for some other work. Your contractor has been saying this, maybe not in so many words. Since you are confined to the shed, you may not be aware of all this…'

'No, no, I am aware of all this. Did you and the girl go to work at the kiln on the eastern side?'

'Yes, and there your girl had a fainting spell. All the men there were new. "Who is this sick creature?" they all asked. "Why should such creatures come here? Is it to fall into the river and die?" I couldn't take this nonsense from him. Some men from our bank joined me. I gave him a fitting reply. I told him that she was the daughter of Vallamedu Angusami mestiri…' Damodaran's face was flushed.

'Times have changed and things are out of our control… One's father may be a big guy and one may see him twirling a manly moustache. But work is work. Or one should stay at home. Instead of understanding this, you proclaim that she is so-and-so's daughter...All this is not practical. Do you know my standing in the river bank today? It's better that I leave the place before I trip on my feet and fall...' said Angusami.

'To top it all, father worries that I have not been married off. If I too spread a mat and lie down, it will be too good indeed,' said Panki from the dark kitchen corner, without the slightest trace of reproach in her voice.

'Damodaran, tell that ill-fated creature to keep her mouth shut and her person far away...One would think that she is holding this house on her shoulders, as though the sun won't rise on the morrow without her. Tell that corpse that no dog need earn even a paisa for me...the proud blood of Pandiya Nadu flows in these veins...This body will always work to feed itself...It is not the species that scavenges on leftovers...'

'I don't know why Anna is saying this and that and hurling words at her...What precisely did she say that was wrong? She has respect for you as her father...'

'I get it now. It's you who has influenced her, so she wags her tongue. You remember one thing about me...You don't seem to have understood me at all after all these years... Even if I am maimed and have lost the use of an arm, I shall eke out an existence using the other. No dog need do anything for me.'

'Anna should forgive us youngsters for acting like they know a lot when he is rightly perturbed by the turn of things... I shall go to my room and light the lamp,' said Damodaran, leaving quickly because he did not want to make matters worse.

Twenty-seven

Was Panki paying him back for the disgust and hatred he had shown towards her all these days and years? Since he had hit the bed with his illness, it had been Panki's earnings that had kept him going.

All things considered, Damodaran was an outsider. Did Panki really owe him anything? She pitied him and hence, earned money for his sake. And he accepted it without demur. This is why she had the temerity to point out that she was an earning member of the household. Was Panki taunting him indirectly for his inability to earn?

'Tangammai, you should have lived, I should have gone. Then we wouldn't have had to face this insult. Why am I not the proud Pandiya Nadu man any more before that girl...?'

❖

'Tangammai, it's quite dark. You've still not lit the lamp in the niche.' Angusami spoke in a loud voice as he returned home from the riverfront. Panki was also with him. She quickly went into the house, fetched the matchbox and lit the lamp. Instantly, she went to her mother, who lay on the mat.

'Your body is hot…Are you running a fever?' she asked, as she touched her body. She quickly went out and told Angusami that her mother's body was hot.

'Fever? Tangammai has a fever?' He entered the room after changing into fresh clothes, taking care not to reveal that he was perturbed. He touched her gently and felt the fever raging in her body. Tangammai screwed up her eyes, unable to bear the light. She looked at Angusami as one would at a stranger. She then looked at Panki.

'Amma, shall I give you some warm water to drink?'

'Tangam, since when have you got this fever? Is your head aching? Shall I bring the doctor?'

'Nothing, for now. I have a bad headache. Suddenly I got a fever and couldn't open my eyes…all I know is that I lay down. I am not aware of how the day turned into night. Did you come back just now? Something is hammering between my eyebrows and the top of my head…'

Tangammai spoke with difficulty. 'There is some palm jaggery in the pot. Add some crushed pepper and water to it and heat it. It will feel good to drink it…Tell her…'

Panki stepped into the kitchen. She had recently begun to work at the riverfront at Damodaran's insistence. She used to spend her time pottering about at home or chatting with the girls in the neighbourhood and roaming around the woods, grazing the goat. She would pluck and taste a variety of fruits, which would give her stomach aches and result in a round of scolding from Tangammai. One day, all of a sudden, she 'grew up'. She could no longer be permitted to wander all over the place with the goat, declared Tangammai.

'All that is between you and your daughter,' said Angusami, distancing himself from the subject.

'So she should go anywhere she pleased as though declaring that she had no father, only her mother?'

'Yes. Do you expect me to tell you what to do about her?'

Damodaran intervened as the two squabbled, and proposed a solution. 'Don't talk just as you please in front of a grown-up girl. Many girls of her age work on the pier. Let Panki also come. Since I'll be there, I can take care of her.'

'Yes, everything falls into place. All that remains for me to do is to make it public on the riverfront that she is my daughter, with a stamp on her to that effect.'

'Anything she does is unacceptable to you. She is wrong if she stays at home, wrong if she goes out... Does she, too, not need a way out?' Tangammai echoed Damodaran's words, though she did not intend to.

'Then do one thing – without further ado, marry this girl,' said Angusami and laughed loudly.

'If one were allowed to marry one's own sister, I would. Just because she is grown up now, should I marry her? Is man not different from animals...?' Damodaran said with great self-control, keeping his head bent low.

'I know all that... If the girl had even slightly better looks, all this reasoning would have flown to the other shore,' said Angusami in a rather harsh tone.

Damodaran began to weep when he heard this. 'So, that's all my brother knows about me, a person he regarded as his own sibling.'

Angusami and Tangammai felt upset. Panki controlled her sobs. Tangammai consoled him. 'Damodara, so this is proof of how much of a man you are. Wipe your eyes...'

But Damodaran continued to sob. 'So, that's all that my brother knows about me.'

'Brother, don't weep,' said Panki. She could say no more and began to weep, distressed by Damodaran's tears. Tangammai's eyes also filled with tears.

Angusami felt guilty. But he was clueless about how to make amends.

Twenty-eight

The doctor felt Tangammai's pulse and recommended a herbal decoction and an ointment to be applied on the forehead. The herbal decoction consisted of the root of kuruntotti, dried ginger and koduveli, while the tumbai leaf and elephant's tooth had to be ground with milk and applied on the forehead. On the seventh day, the fever came down. But her body was covered with tiny 'pearls' – she had contracted smallpox.

Tangammai lay in bed. Angusami stayed at home to help her. Panki and Damodaran went to the river. 'You don't have to stay at home and feel upset about me. Let Panki stay at home. You will feel better,' Tangammai told Angusami.

'Tangam, I cannot bear to leave you. Even if I went there, I wouldn't be able to stay put. I'd be constantly thinking of you and your aches and pains…it is better that I stay at home, looking after you…'

'I don't like that. The Mother goddess has given me five or six pearls. In a few days, she will take them back…Since the fever has subsided, there is nothing the matter with me... I tell you honestly,' said Tangammai with a wan smile on her face.

In one week, Tangammai's body was fully covered with pearl-sized pustules. 'These are "black pearls". The Mother should be kind and take them away...' The doctor's voice trailed off as he spoke.

'If you speak like this being the doctor, how are we to console ourselves?' Angusami asked, deeply distressed.

'There is nothing to be achieved now by hoping or despairing. All this is a game for the goddess... Just a few marks here and there on the face as marks of her visit... That's all right. Nothing is in our hands. Just keep praying to the goddess... It is not something to grieve about.' As he conveyed his inability to help in the matter, the doctor went down the stairs.

Angusami sat at Tangammai's bedside all the time, like a crazed person. This was the first time in his life that he had felt real sorrow, as far as he could remember, and it threw him completely off balance. He lit joss sticks, poured fresh coconut water into her mouth, fanned her body with sprigs of neem. Every minute, he asked her about how she felt.

'That's manly, indeed, getting so upset... There's nothing wrong with me. The goddess is testing me. I am sure that Lord Anjaneya will ensure that no harm comes to me. You should not neglect yourself and fall ill. It's no use, my living, if you fall ill. There can be a picture only if there is a wall on which to draw... Even the doctor said that this pox is a type that passes...'

Angusami was silent. He did not understand why all this was happening to him. 'What harm did I cause anyone?' And

Tangammai – she would not hurt a fly.

A gust of wind blew in from the grove. The dark green branches of the tamarind, mango and jackfruit trees swayed in the wind, spreading their branches. The coconut fronds also swayed wildly. The mynahs, sparrows and their friends sat on the manjanatti branches and chirped a hundred tunes. A raven cawed unmusically from the top of a kanjira tree. In a corner of the grove, the tethered goat bleated in fear. Perhaps two snakes had entwined themselves with each other and were fighting…And outside the stone wall, in the police lines, one could see the transcendental Hanuman on the white wall, with a benign expression…It had been days since he had seen the picture and it did not form clearly in his mind…It turned shapeless, vanished, reshaped itself in strange ways…Why?…The Hanuman temple was not far from the house. One went up a bit and then down, and could see it on the other side of the wall. Though it was within hailing distance, he had never wished to go there and revive old memories…Perhaps because it was so near…Surely, this wasn't the most important thing to be thinking about now?

The grove, the surrounding greenery – nothing was available for their use now. When Tangammai's father had died, the few privileges that had been theirs, thanks to his familiarity with the authorities, had gone away with him. They even paid a rent for the house.

Does everything get destroyed and reappear? Why did Tangammai contract this illness? What changes was it supposed to occasion?

Nothing was permanent in this world. One shouldn't love anybody or anything too much. He had neither coveted, nor longed for anything ever since he was a boy. He did not even remember his mother with affection. Mother was just a thought, she was faceless. He had no 'native town' either. His past began in the marketplace, its contours were rough-hewn. Preceding this was darkness, only darkness. He had one motivating impulse during his life in the streets of the market – that of assuaging his hunger. Once he could see beyond this, he could picture a different life for himself, Tangammai entered his life, filled his heart and soul. When Tangammai held out her love, unspoken, the seed of love germinated in him, unknown to him earlier. And she was his all – he had lost himself to her. And that cause, that woman, was today...

Tangammai recovered, belying Angusami's extreme despair...

'Dear man, I am sure that the goddess is kind to you. And god's grace is with you. Till date, no one has survived a pox attack lasting twenty-eight days. Now your wife has some deep pockmarks, that's all. There is no fever and tomorrow is the thirty-second day. She can have a bath,' said the doctor. Tangammai, who used to look like a carved idol earlier, now looked like a tarnished statue. Her face was like a sieve, what with the pockmarks. The tip of her nose seemed to have been snipped off...She felt weak and her body had given way. She reminded one of a banana tree shorn of its bunches of fruit. When she smiled, her gums looked redder than usual and her smile looked unreal.

'I can cope with any loss...Tangammai should live,' had been the constant refrain on Angusami's lips. He was not unduly perturbed by Tangammai's appearance.

Their tiny house was suffused with a new glow the day Tangammai took a bath after her illness. Everyone was smiling. Panki would not allow Damodaran to head straight to his room after work.

'Stay, Anna. Mother had her bath today and father got prasada from the temple. He lit a lamp for Madan Tampuran and laid a garland of red flowers before the god. Everything changed for father when mother fell ill... Stay put. Don't go,' said Panki, cleaning the blackened glass sleeve of the hurricane lamp.

'Very well. You light the lamp, I'm waiting.'

'The bronze lamp has been cleaned and polished to a shine and has already been lit. Father and mother are mumbling among themselves in front of the lamp. They may be reciting prayers or just talking in whispers... quite like a newly-wed couple!'

'Hear that now... from an old woman who has seen umpteen newly-weds!' Damodaran teased Panki.

'Who's there, talking about us?' Tangammai's feeble voice reached them.

'Tangammai, don't bother to raise your voice. They are young people... Let them talk and pass the time,' said Angusami in a low voice.

'It's only now that father seems to have become normal... One can understand that mother was ill so she stayed away from food and drink. Father neither ate, nor slept... neither washed, nor bathed. He was like a crazed man...'

'Anna is like that – that's his nature. If he likes someone, he'll smother that person with affection. If he dislikes someone, he won't give that person a second look.'

'Do you have to tell me all this, as though I don't know it already... The way he treats her and the way he treats me says it all...'

Panki offered Damodaran some payasam on a piece of

banana leaf. It was a sweet occasion for all four.

The following day, as soon as the sun went down, Tangammai began to shiver a little.

'You have not moved around for a long time and had a bath after a long gap. I suppose that's why you feel a bit low after sundown. Don't get worried. Nothing that we need to worry about will happen.' Angusami spoke in a reassuring tone, but he was afraid within.

Someone seemed to call out to him when he had fallen asleep, around midnight. He got up in a trice and went towards Tangammai, who was sleeping close by, on a mat.

'Tangam . . . Tangamme . . .' he called out. There was no movement, no word from Tangammai. He raised the wick of the hurricane lamp for more light and looked again. Tangammai's story was over. 'Tangamme . . .' Angusami screamed from the pit of his stomach. He remembered that scream.

Twenty-nine

When everything was over, what was left for him, Angusami thought over and over... What was left?

Pure hatred... That was all that remained.

The more he reflected, the clearer it became to him that his life was a huge emptiness. Life with Tangammai – that short span of time had got over in the wink of an eye. And that brief moment alone gave a meaning to a life that was being lived for so many years. And now...

'Panki says that you have not been your usual self since the fracture... That you have neither any interest, nor any enthusiasm for anything,' Damodaran began.

'Look here, I cannot revert to my youth. Once you have eaten off it, you call a banana leaf a dirty leaf. It has to be thrown out. One can drink a medicine to cure an illness. Is there any medicine for death? One cannot drink poison. So one has to live out the destined time.'

'Yes, but I want to know the reason for this sense of loss and exhaustion that has gripped you...'

'You know it very well but still you ask, in one way or the other! I am no longer relevant these days...You should marry, live and earn well...That's all that remains to be done, as far as I am concerned.'

'So that's it? I have lived close to my elder brother for so long, although under an adjacent thatch. Panki is like my own sibling, in good times and bad. Tangammai akka left us more than five years ago. As for me, I shall not marry till Panki is married and settled. There is more reason to be concerned about a young woman. I am a man and nobody is going to be unduly bothered about me. I am sure there is a man destined to marry Panki too...'

'Damodara, you are an innocent young man. If I told you to enjoy a plain drink of water, you'd agree to do so...Don't you remember what happened last year, when someone came to see her from Chitraru? How you had a fight with him since he spoke ill of her? A fruit has to ripen by itself...it cannot be ripened by force...'

'So be it.'

'By then, you'll be as grey as me.'

'I am a man. It hardly matters if I am old or grey. First Panki will be taken care of. Only then will I think of myself.'

'Let that be. As for me, I don't want to talk about her. Nor have I anything to give her. Her mother too left her nothing. I get my daily gruel because she toils on the riverfront. And the very thought of it upsets me. Just as I can do nothing for her, you can't either. Aren't you being stupid, intentionally? As for me, I never thought even in my dreams that I'd be dead wood by the time I was fifty...'

'Annan should not fear anything. Till there is breath in this pipe, I shall take care of you. Everything will be just fine.

Fifty years is not to be considered old age. You are going to work for many years, like before. Our Meera Sahib plies his boat even at seventy-six. He still earns his daily bread by working in the river. Should I continue…?'

'To each his own. Meera Sahib's wife is still alive. There are no children at home to bother him. If someone – who is one's own – cooks one a pot of fish curry and rice, one can live up to a hundred with a happy mind. I was all but finished when Tangammai left me. I became an old man that very moment.'

'Had one known that you would be hit so badly, one could have thought of a second marriage. There was no need to feel so depressed.'

'Look here, that's why I say you don't know a Pandiya Nadu man. Is Tangammai to be mentioned in the same breath as another woman? If I had had such thoughts, was there a dearth of women on the riverfront? Life was when I lived with Tangammai. After her, there is nothing, nothing for me. The only reason I do not drive Panki away is that she is Tangammai's daughter, that's all.'

Damodaran searched high and low for a suitable man for Panki. There was a man from the south, from Kaliyakkavilai.

'If the girl can earn, we want nothing by way of bridal gifts. He sells jaggery and such stuff for a living,' said the middleman.

The negotiations took place in the shed. It had already been conveyed to the other party that the girl was not good-looking and hence, would not be 'shown'.

'What's so special about looks? If she is presented before a few people, she shouldn't be spoken ill of, that's all,' the boy's side had responded. Still, when the boy saw Panki, his face clouded over. He got up to leave and told his father to leave too.

'What's this, you are leaving without a word! Weren't you already told about the girl?' Damodaran stood up and asked him.

'But we didn't know that she was a she-devil that gobbled children, an "eenampechi",' said the boy's friend.

'For this thin black pole, you need no less than a princess of the Kaliyakkavilai royalty...' raged Damodaran.

'Don't talk too much. No one can want her. The most convenient thing would be for you yourself to marry her...' The men left without further ado.

Was Panki really his responsibility, wondered Damodaran. Had he bitten off more than he could chew?

'Damodaran Anna, why should you trouble yourself over me? Do I strike you as one who will bear a child if she is not married off this instant?' Panki shed tears as her fingers plied the sand aimlessly.

'Panki, I promised your mother that I'll care for you as a sister. If Tangammai had been alive, I'd have annulled that promise and married you.'

'So...! I now know that there is at least one man that has such a wish!' Panki laughed even as she shed tears.

'I'll try...as much as possible...Otherwise I'll marry you.' Damodaran got up to leave the instant he said this, before Panki could see his face, and merged into the darkness of his room.

Thirty

Panki did not venture to think of a life of her own. Perhaps no man existed to share her life. But there did exist a strong youth willing to spare a thought for her and that steadied her to a large extent.

'Panki is not quite unlucky. As long as Damodaran is around, she need not be married off,' said the women who worked on the riverfront, teasing Panki. Whatever the degree of provocation, Panki never once imagined Damodaran standing by her right, as her husband.

With a true heart, she wished Damodaran would find a pretty and good-natured wife, someone she could lovingly address as 'Chettathi' (big sister). Why did she feel this? Damodaran had even told her once that the heavens would not fall if he married her. But in the depths of her heart, she never could picture him as her man.

No one in the wide world liked her, however lowly he might be. Were she to share the life of that affectionate and pure-hearted man, he would certainly be subjected to derogatory remarks on her account. That was something she could not bear even for an instant. 'All said and done, could you find no better woman than this embodied ugliness?' he'd be told. 'Damodaran is my brother,' she had told herself, till the words stuck hard in her mind.

'This girl is stupid. That man is with her day and night. Is there anything that cannot be done if a woman sets her heart on it?' the woman living near the well would say. Though middle-aged, she liked to line her eyes with kohl. She chewed betel regularly, which lent a tint of red to her lips. Her ears were fully adorned from the top to the lobe and she often clicked her tongue, as though she savoured life as much as one savours good food.

'I have to just tell my husband and he will fetch the moon god from the sky. If there is even a shade of distress in my eyes, he goes haywire. I may be slightly upset about something or the other, but he'll insist on knowing why. Whatever be the problem, he'll insist on finding a solution. And one more thing. From my youth, I've always been like this... taken the trouble to look good. These days you don't have to be like that. You need more guts and smartness. You can pick up Damodaran and the likes of him like one picks flowers.'

All that Panki did in response was to smile at her. 'Wretch, one has to light a lamp to figure out if that was a smile, so attractive are you!' the woman muttered to herself behind Panki's back.

Panki's hours on the riverfront taught her a lot about life and its complexities. She mingled with many women, some of them attractive, and a few who had lived with several men and landed there without any support and with children to feed. If a woman was attractive, she would beguile a male and in turn get beguiled till she was left high and dry with his child. In almost all instances, the hurt party was the woman. Yet no woman was averse to vanity and boasting, qualities that ultimately led them to the depths of despair. Above all, she knew that the roof she slept under belonged to a good man, and that sufficed for her.

Panki was proud of Damodaran, whose heart was clean and who behaved well. She forgot her pain when she addressed him as her brother, with much affection, as her innate right. She did not think that her marriage was a big problem, all said and done. 'Annan and father should not bother about it at all. If I am destined to marry, it has to happen,' she would often say.

Thirty-one

'Damodara, one can't leave everything to fate and wait one's turn. Either we stop the work we do here now and go elsewhere to dredge sand, or we can go and break stones. If we depend on the river, we can only starve and perish.'

'Brother, you can say anything, but don't say that we'll starve to death if we believe that the river will give us a living. We acted against time-tested practices. We did the wrong things. We strengthened the banks with stone walls. We demolished Madan's platform and pushed the idol a mile away into the interior. There are lorry sheds where we once heaped hillocks of sand. All our boats have gone to the eastern part. Jobs, market, coir-making, everything is big there. The unthinkable happened, like a sleight of hand. Chokkan the monkey, divided the bread well and the event is now old hat. Well, it is no use ruing what is no longer there. I am thinking of working for a building contractor. I am here only because of Panki. I manage to get some work at the kiln across the river. Once the rains come, it will be risky to cross the river.

One will have to take the bridge and walk thrice the distance to reach the kiln... True, things have changed, as you just said...'

'Damodara, what I say, I say after due thought. Without so much as a whisper, the contractor dismantled the shed overnight. Whatever I have received due to his kindness is gone. But for this rotting corpse of a girl, I too would have gone... to wherever these legs took me...'

'Anna, why such words? I am determined to find a way for Panki. Stay at home and eat whatever we manage to get. Something is bound to happen. When the wind changes direction, the sailboat also does...'

When he was ill and laid up in bed, there was a reason for him to stay at home. Even then, he felt that he was being held back by a leash. Now there was nothing before him... except time and emptiness.

It was meaningless to confine himself to one spot and brood about a past, while his life waned incessantly. He ought to do something or the other, he felt. But when he got down to doing that something, he was taken over by weakness and debility. A familiar disappointment gripped him.

Once he went for a walk in the market, as he was bored of sitting at home. A large number of friends and acquaintances began to enquire about his well-being.

'Is that our Angusami? You have greyed and become an old man. What is this stiffness in your arm? Arthritis? Well, you are not too young... It's best to stay at home...'

This was the majority opinion.

'Angusami is seasoned wood. He can lift this sack with one hand,' came a second opinion, a teaser of sorts.

'He is an old man... Imagine expecting him to lift that

huge gunny bag! It is a thing of the past.' Everyone laughed.

Nothing was like old times. Even the market street had changed. The old roofs used to be low and one had to bend one's head to get in. Those roofs were gone, as were the oil-fed chain lamps. There were electric tube lights and rows of cemented flat-roofed shops. There were colourful advertisement boards. Red government buses, crowded with people, plied to and fro. There were no rows of ox-carts carrying loads from the pier. Goods came in big lorries. Men and women wore silk clothes and rode in colourful motor cars. The good old mundu and cotton towel were hardly to be seen.

As he sat at home, the more he brooded, the more intolerable the changes became. The grove was no longer covered with its old lush green canopy. The old and dried up trees on the other side of the wall had been chopped down. The sun radiated white heat from the whitewashed Hanuman temple, highlighting an empty lot devoid of trees and bushes. It was rumoured that a new police training college was to be constructed. Once that happened, his present home and Damodaran's thatch were bound to be pulled down.

Even such a state of deprivation was welcome. Let that too happen. Everything changed but he was going to be his same old self. No one sensed this change in him. No one near him was so weak, so tired. Everyone went to work, everyone worked hard, sweating it out. Everyone laughed, spent money, mingled with one another. All of them ate, took pleasure in things, snored and slept without a care in the world.

Panki was sound asleep in the house. In the evening, after the two had returned home, Damodaran had come in after changing into clean clothes, his hair oiled and combed.

During their usual chat, Panki contributed her mite every now and then when Damodaran spoke. As the rice gruel boiled, its smell wafted into the air, mixing with the acrid smoke issuing from the faggots. Angusami controlled the cough flaring his nostrils. He took a beedi from Damodaran, lit it up and began to puff.

'Anna, did Panki tell you what work we did today?' began Damodaran. 'Did Panki tell you anything?' That was how their chats began these days. 'You know, we left early today but there was not a single boat at the pier. There was not a single bullock cart or lorry. We crossed to the other bank and went to the brick kiln. But the bricks were not baked. It would take three days, said the contractor, Pushkaran. We had almost decided to return home, empty-handed, like yesterday. Just then, loads of tapioca arrived from the Periya Ela fields. The tapioca had to be sent to Karakulam, across the river. The man calculated that it would be cheaper to send it across by boat rather than have it transported by head loads. He told us that he would pay us a rupee and a quarter per load. We carried the tapioca and loaded it in Kochappi Panikkar's boat. Before it was noon, we had unloaded the stuff on the Karakulam bank. We got twelve rupees and we paid one-and-a-half rupees for hiring the boat. So we have ten-and-a-half rupees and some tapioca... We have money to spend for two days... Let's not worry now about how many more days we'll have to do this... We'll certainly accept what has been doled out to us by god...'

'That tapioca is useless. I put it on the fire as soon as I came back, but it is still not done,' said Panki.

Everything takes its destined course... Everything was accumulating in his mind like the soot that accumulates in the glass sleeve of the hurricane lamp...

Somewhere a dog barked. Across, in the police compound, the bats indulged in a screeching contest around the temple. The punnai tree was still there...

On one occasion, in the middle of the night, he and Tangammai had been near that tree... No, to hell with those old memories, this sadness... Why bring them to mind?

Sleep eluded him.

Thirty-two

The months of May and June were dry. The rains began in the second half of July, first as a slight sprinkle, which was nothing much to speak of.

The sky darkened slowly. Suddenly the sun shone brightly and a few drops fell, like streaks of glass. The sky turned a spotless blue again, for two days. In the evening, it turned black, bringing on an instant night, and the rain descended with a huge noise.

It poured and thundered through the night and paused a little before noon. The clouds once again gathered from all sides and began to pour with a demonic force. The ground started to swell up. The rain continued at a relentless pace, making naught of night, dawn, day and dusk.

The paths and open spaces of the town became a river of swirling water. At Vallamedu, the meeting point of the rivers, the waters seethed and swelled, swirling and decimating anything that came in the way, like a vengeful tigress. The banks, the town, everything was the river.

The trees and the proud coconut palms resembled women covered in burqas, their heads hanging down. Their heads had lost their leafy thatches and looked like wet poultry birds.

'Damodaran, is this an announcement of doomsday? It is demonic, this rain. The northern wall of the house is dripping, which has created a pond inside. I had wanted to thatch the roof anew two months ago. But my arm became accursed. Am I able to do anything? Everything has come to a standstill...'

'Why say all this now? Of what use is it? We can weave the thatch only when the rain stops. Leave that aside... One should eat one's food at the right time... Did Panki cook something?'

'Ask her yourself,' said Angusami. Panki was throwing out water that had collected in vessels from the leaks. Her clothes were completely wet.

'Not bad, not bad at all...! Have you drenched yourself so that you don't forget your occupation of dipping yourself into the river and dredging sand?'

Panki turned her head abruptly. Damodaran was standing at the kitchen door, laughing.

'So when did Anna come? In what state is your room? Is it leaking?'

'I came here because it is bad there and it is the same here, I see. Two more such days and we too will end up in the school buildings, like the people living in the river valley.'

'It won't be bad if we have to move. We can at least get some gruel to drink. We can stay put.'

'Thankfully, we are not fated to eat off charity.'

'Who knows about fate? It has been days since I boiled anything here.'

'But yesterday, Annan said that you had made gruel and

that he drank it.'

'How's that possible? It's months since father earned anything. It's what you and I earn that gets us the food. Just count – today is the fifth day that we haven't gone to work...'

'Still, we don't have to long for free gruel. I'll be back in just a while.' Damodaran went away abruptly.

'Anna, can't you go when the rain abates a bit? We don't have an umbrella and the grass hat is torn badly...'

'If we think about avoiding getting wet in the rain, we will all starve...' Damodaran's voice was loud enough to be heard by Angusami. He stepped into the red slush on the path, displacing the accumulated pools.

Angusami had experienced many a rainy season on the riverfront. Never had it been so furious, so frightening. It was the same sound, of pouring rain, that he heard from morning till he went to sleep, tired out. The same sound pounded on the roof and filled the grove when his sleep gave way, all of a sudden.

'Brother, what sort of rain is this? Years ago, there had been a similar season and floods, when our Kiliyaru bridge broke. This time, the rain is going to be even worse. Today was the sixth day I remained in the house. I went out to see how things were, after much thought. Have you seen how the river and the pier look? One has to dive and find where the bank is. One more foot of water and the bridge will be drowned.'

Meera Sahib was shivering as he stepped in, his clothes totally wet.

'Sahib, why did you venture out in this weather? How did your wife allow you to step out of the house?' said Angusami, laughing.

'If one stays rooted at home, listening to the wife, who is going to buy the rice for the gruel?'

'So you decided to venture out in this driving rain and go as far as the Kottar rice market near Kanyakumari, I suppose!'

'Well, it is different for you. You can live like an elder who gets a pension. The daughter and the young man will take care of you. You are a lucky fellow…'

'It's hardly like you think. It's been three days since we cooked any gruel. The boy and the girl are here…but he is not an owner of groves that he can hack off coconuts and walk home. Our hearths are lit only when we go to the river…'

Thirty-three

The rain had destroyed all that it could. It had reduced itself to a drizzle, as though it was contemplating letting up. The floodplain looked like a wound oozing blood and pus. Water covered the fields and the flood shimmered like a wide sea unto the horizon. On the tall jackfruit tree near the brick kiln, a row of crows sat, cawing loudly, flapping their wings and smoothing their feathers. A crow lay dead in the slush near the unbaked bricks. The mimosa tree appeared to have bent down to offer its condolences to the dead birds and its branches seemed to be in a swoon.

Near the wall of the bridge, the ferry boat lay tethered like a lone orphan, filled with the muddy river water. Damodaran went to the bridge and looked around him. The rains had wrought total destruction. Few men were visible on the main road. Every now and then, lorries rushed away with people headed for relief camps. The sand bank was covered with rainwater and a few buffaloes were wallowing in it. Dragonflies flew about, smelling the muddy waters and darting off into the distance, without a second thought. Crows swooped down and sat on the horns of buffaloes and flew off, only to descend again.

Angusami threw away the beedi he was puffing at and got up eagerly as Damodaran came up the steps.

'Tell me, the rain is subsiding now – is there any work for us? One cannot cross to the other side.'

Panki brought Damodaran a dry towel. 'Take off your wet clothes Anna, use this.'

'It has been raining for so many days. It is only today that it has turned into a drizzle. So things are hardly normal and the news is not good. We haven't seen anything out here since we are at a distance from the bank. There is not a single hut left in the floodplain and the valley. People have moved into schools and cinema halls. One cannot cross over to the other bank for at least another week. The ferry is full of slush and water. And who knows when the river will calm down and the eddies and whirlpools will disappear? Only then can we think of working.'

'These are the times of Death. I don't recall seeing such merciless rain or such starvation. Did you manage to have some tea or something?'

'One side of his shop has collapsed. So Pushkaran has closed down his tea shop. There is the shop at Melakkarai... but where is the money?'

'That wretch has managed to get a vessel from somewhere... Pledge it or sell it and scrape through for a few days. How much longer can we starve?'

The pouring rain had stopped, but not the drizzle. There was a thick cloud cover and the sky rumbled.

'If it continues this way, what are we to do? We could go

to the pier... We could go to the other side and look for work, like digging or other such work...' began Panki.

'Wretch! Shut your big mouth and mind your own business. One should weed you out from the root and put you into a pit. Only then will I be free from your curse. And that poor fellow will have a way out,' snapped Angusami.

'Anna, why do you talk like this? The poor girl, what can she do? I too have been watching the scene since the day I came here.'

'Ei, you shut your trap. As long as this one lives, there is no hope for me or you. Tangammai left... like a vessel of water that broke and spilt before one's thirst was quenched. What's left of me? This creature will calm down only when this flightless bird goes up in smoke. Let no one ever talk about me.'

'Why keep chewing my raw flesh? If I am a burden, I ought to be gone. The river has fed me so far. I can go into the same river. You'll be free of trouble...'

'Wretched corpse, go. Go now, and who are you trying to scare?'

'Anna, can't you be quiet? You always tell everyone that an intelligent man should use his tongue sparingly. She is a woman... She may be upset about many things. At times, she may talk without knowing what she's saying.'

'Come what may, I am the wrongdoer. I should have gone away as soon as Tangammai died... I was concerned... That's why things have come this far...'

The air was thick with unspoken accusations, disappointments and hostility. They could go to work at the kiln the following day, Damodaran cut in. The ovens and sheds had been repaired and they were looking for men. Though the river was still flowing over the banks, the current was not too strong. It was decided that they would cross by boat. A few men were to join them down the river. Panki forgot her trials and tribulations for the time being and slept in the hope of a better dawn.

Thirty-four

Everyone was at the river at the crack of dawn. Angusami too had joined them for he could not bear another day of lonely incarceration at home. 'Father should not try to do something that does not suit his health. It is still cold. He should wear this dry waist cloth,' said Panki, taking out one from the box as they prepared to leave.

Though the rain had stopped, the sky was not yet clear. Damodaran untied the boat and cast his eyes on the immense expanse of water. 'Anna, it does not look easy to me. I think the current is pretty strong still. The wind is blowing eastward and it feels wet. Even a shower on top of the hill will cause a flood in minutes. I shall go alone and check it out. Then we will all cross. Or cross the bridge and walk around the valley. We'll need to walk a bit, that's all.'

'You are easily scared, I must say. There's a slight breeze, there's less rain. There won't be flash floods. It's our own river. Don't we all know its currents and eddies and how to tackle them? Push the boat, don't dither. Get in, all of you.

Or are you all scared?' said Angusami, seating himself on the cross-board at the prow.

'It's years since I felt the touch of a boat,' said Angusami as he felt a thrill grip his body. The others stepped in, one by one, keen to avoid being labelled cowardly by him.

'Get in, get in, Annan thinks everything is like old times... It's our river...but everything is upside down...That he does not understand...When a new flood recedes, it takes some time to assess how the deeper channels flow... Panki, why are you waiting? Get in. I am ready,' said Damodaran. He pushed the boat and got in. She looked at him with deep affection and jumped in after him.

An easterly wind blew strong and cold. The sky had lightened in the east and a dull light was pervading it. Two cranes flew above, heading in the opposite direction in apparently purposeful flight and disappeared.

The boat moved smoothly as Damodaran plied it, all alone. 'Seat yourselves properly, balancing the two sides. The boat is tilting to the left a bit,' shouted Damodaran, plunging the pole into the water.

'Don't shout. It won't tilt. Do your job properly...Hold the pole properly,' shot back Angusami.

A huge black cloud rose up in the eastern sky and hid the sun. It grew larger and larger, the tentative light of the morning faded and the river's waters flowed in a darker hue.

Just as Damodaran had feared, the current was strong midstream. He manoeuvred the pole with all his strength to steady the boat, but the inner flow was too powerful. 'It's too tough. It would be good if somebody joined me...' Even as Damodaran said this, the boat turned around in a circle. 'Hold, hold!' two men stood up to help him.

Panki and two other women screamed as Damodaran fell into the river in the wink of an eye, along with the pole. The boat swirled once more and turned upside down. There was a deafening silence for a while. The curtain of black clouds parted a little, revealing a veiled sun. Far in the distance, someone shouted, 'The boat has capsized midstream!' and ran up the bridge.

A crowd collected in no time and there was much hustle and bustle. Beneath the bridge, the water flowed full and fast.

'The flow is strong. If we go to the pier downstream, we may catch the men. They are men who know the river. If they escape the inner eddies, they will swim to safety.' The crowd rushed towards Kizhakkarai. Hours went by. There was little light. The people in the crowd became concerned when they realized that Angusami and Damodaran were among the men in the boat.

'It's strange that such men got into a boat when they knew that the eddies would be strong now. Even a newborn knows that, when there is a flood. How did these two agree to this?'

'Whoever it may be – this elder or the one we hold in high regard for his experience – he will act wisely only if his stars are right... Should we step in and search now? First we have to watch for heads above the water...'

A little later, Damodaran clambered up, exhausted. He was in no condition to talk.

'There were six... are we all here...?' asked Damodaran, straining hard to sound coherent.

'Everybody will be here. Don't get flustered. You have swallowed too much water.'

Soon, three men, including Angusami, reached the bank. Two women followed them.

One person was missing.

'How many women?'

'Three.'

'One has to be born to make it three. Who is the third one?'

'Is Panki there?' yelled Damodaran.

'Panki?' Angusami looked all around him, his senses returning to him.

... Water was swirling around over his head. He swallowed gulps of water, held his breath and kicked his feet, trying hard to emerge to the surface. At that moment, someone pulled his feet in a desperate act, an act of life in the face of death. The basic animal instinct in him drove him to kick hard... It was a woman's body, he knew, as strands of hair got stuck between his toes. All this took a brief moment, but the fear for his very life lasted a full minute! Angusami surfaced, wondering how he had overcome his handicap... Now he was on the bank... That was his last thought.

'Panki, so that was you!'

The crowd talked about the foolishness of the men's venture and each voiced their thoughts on the matter.

'In this sort of season, even if there is a pause in the rain, a man who knows the river well will never venture on to a boat. When a man decides to be self-willed, we cannot find fault with the river... How stupid these men have been.'

'That poor girl, Panki... She's not to be seen.'

'Panki? Mooppan's daughter?'

Damodaran lay on the bank, babbling. He was confused and not in his senses.

Angusami was fully conscious. He knew Panki would not return.

'It is going to rain again,' someone said.

Angusami looked at the sky. In the western horizon, black clouds were rising and gathering, growing ever larger.

A group of crows flew southward in a hurry, imagining the sudden darkness to be the onset of night.

The river flowed past, unaffected by the tragedy enacted on its bank, majestic with the swell of flood above and the secret eddies below, carrying with it the completion of one more life story.

www.ingramcontent.com/pod-product-compliance
Ingram Content Group UK Ltd.
Pitfield, Milton Keynes, MK11 3LW, UK
UKHW041347190726
13845UKWH00026B/458

9 789352 907526